EYE FOR REVENGE

MARGARET MONTAGUE

CHERYL BRADSHAW

Eye For Revenge
A Margaret Montague Mystery

New York Times & USA Today Bestselling Author
CHERYL BRADSHAW

"Adhere to your purpose and you will soon feel as well as you ever did. On the contrary, if you falter, and give up, you will lose the power of keeping any resolution, and will regret it all your life."

-Abraham Lincoln

PROLOGUE

Margaret Montague hummed a familiar tune as she moved from bookcase to bookcase, using her feather duster to ensure her in-house library was spotless before the afternoon guests arrived. At age seventy-two, she thought she would have sold Montague Manor by now, but every time the thought crossed her mind she tucked it away, deciding the timing wasn't right.

One day, perhaps.

Margaret had owned the turn-of-the-century bed and breakfast for over thirty years. In that time, she'd come to feel like family to some of the guests who returned year after year, often choosing to stay in the same room when they visited. It had been three long years since her dear husband, Oliver, had passed away. And though not a single day went by when her thoughts didn't turn to him, her guests, with their cheery dispositions and chatty repartee, had made life a lot more bearable.

The manor had six suites in total, each decorated in the theme of a famous author's works. There was the William Shakespeare, the Edgar Allan Poe, the Jane Austen, the Ernest

Hemingway, the Emily Dickinson, and last but not least, the Agatha Christie, Margaret's personal favorite.

The sound from the chimes hanging on the front doorknob indicated the guest she'd been waiting for had arrived. Margaret slipped her feather duster into the storage closet and scurried toward the front of the house. The young woman who'd just entered the reception area was tall and slender. Her long, dark hair had been swept up into a loose bun, the stray curls cascading over the sides of her face, highlighting her cat-shaped green eyes.

The woman tucked a few locks of hair behind her ear and looked up, half-smiling when she made eye contact with Margaret.

"You must be Natalie," Margaret said. "You booked a two-night stay in the Austen suite, correct?"

Natalie nodded as she looked around. "Am I the only guest this week or are there others?"

"Oh, there's a few of you. I expect you'll meet them at breakfast tomorrow morning."

"I skip breakfast most days. I hope that's not a problem?"

"Not at all," Margaret said with a swish of her hand, "though it's been said my quiche is the best in town. If you change your mind, or if you prefer eating later in the day, I can set aside a plate for you. Just let me know."

"Thanks, I will."

"Let's show you to your room, then, shall we?"

Margaret headed toward the staircase, and Natalie followed her.

"I love the way you've decorated the place," Natalie said.

"Me too." Margaret turned to see her peeking inside the Shakespeare room. "I take it you're a reader. Most who stay at the manor are."

"I've been reading since I was a child. I even worked in the school library in junior high."

"What genre of books strike your fancy, dear?"

Natalie tapped a finger to the side of her face, thinking. "I suppose it depends on my mood. One day it's a classic; the next, a romantic suspense."

Speaking of moods, Margaret found Natalie a bit melancholy. She sensed something was amiss, but given they'd just met, she decided not to question her on the matter—for now.

Reaching the Austen suite, Margaret pushed the French doors all the way open, flipping the switch to the crystal chandelier. "Here we are. I hope you'll find it to your liking."

"Oh my." Natalie entered the room and spun around. "It's like I've stepped back in time. It's perfect."

"I'm glad you approve."

The Jane Austen suite was decorated in shades of grayish-blue and cream, with gold and bronze accents throughout. On the opposite end of the room, beside the wrought-iron bed, a window seat of cushiony velvet created the perfect reading nook and a view of the majestic courtyard garden outside. Next to the nook was an upright piano. On the wall above it, a pair of bronze wall sconces adorned each side of a collection of framed quotes from Austen's books. A wood, round, antique accent table beside the piano held one of Margaret's favorite highlights of the room—an arrangement for afternoon high tea. Today's offering included a sampling of teas atop a bronze, two-tiered tray filled with goodies—a scone and jam with clotted cream, a crustless sandwich cut into four pieces, and two slices of cake.

Pressing a hand to her chest, Natalie said, "Wow, you've thought of everything."

"I aim to keep my guests comfortable and happy."

Natalie crossed the room, sat on the window seat, and took in the view of the garden. She said nothing for a time, and Margaret wondered whether she should excuse herself, leaving Natalie to settle in. She'd decided to do just that when she saw something that gave her pause—Natalie flicking a couple of tears off her cheek.

Margaret cleared her throat. "Would you like me to go so you can get unpacked?"

"Oh, no, I ... it's been a rough few days. It's the reason I'm here. I needed space, time to think, away from my college room-mate, Bronte. We've been friends since elementary school. But now ... now, I'm thinking maybe we shouldn't have moved in together."

"Having a friendship as long as that is special. I'm sure you can work things out. Can't you?"

Natalie shrugged. "I don't know. We've always done almost everything together, but now she spends most of her time with Miles, her boyfriend. He's at our apartment all the time, plops right down in between the two of us when we're watching *our* shows, eats *our* snacks without even asking. It's annoying."

Margaret shuffled across the room, joining Natalie at the window seat. "Have you talked to Bronte about how you're feeling?"

"I've never been any good at confrontation. I'll admit, I've been giving the silent treatment. I know it's not a healthy way to go about it. She keeps asking me what's wrong, and I feel like she should know me well enough to figure it out without me having to tell her. Seems obvious to me."

"If Bronte isn't clear about what the problem is, she won't know how to fix it."

Natalie blew out a long sigh. "I suppose you're right."

"Lifelong friends are hard to come by, take it from me. If you've always been close, you can't let a little squabble over her boyfriend ruin the bond between you."

"I just ... I don't know what to do."

Margaret stood. "Come with me. I believe I have just the thing you need."

"You do?"

Margaret nodded, and Natalie followed her to the library, gasping when she entered. "Whoa, this is amazing. I had no idea you had a library in the manor."

"I don't post any photos of it on the website. I like the element of surprise in some things—and this is one of them. My guest's reactions when they see it ... well, it never disappoints."

"May I borrow a book or two while I'm here?"

"Any book you like." Margaret reached over, picking a book off the shelf and placing it in Natalie's hands. "Have you ever heard of *Eye for Revenge*?"

"I haven't."

"I think you'd like it. There's a little bit of murder, a little bit of romance, and a little of something else. Read it, you'll see ..."

EYE FOR REVENGE

1

Evie Richelle soared down the cracked sidewalk, legs spread, rubber tires spinning. Summer was here at last, fanning a warm breeze through the air that slapped her uncombed, blond locks against her face like willows in the wind. Her new Roadmaster Aerobee Renegade bike was everything she'd wanted, only it wasn't new. It was something her Grandma Ruby called "vintage." Eleven-year-old Evie didn't know what the word "vintage" meant, and she didn't care either. As far as she was concerned, it was *cool*. And cool suited her just fine.

Tough and yellow, the bike had a brawny bee painted on its side. But the bee wasn't what Evie loved most. It was the way the wide handlebars curved down at the ends. When her fingers wound around the stiff, rubber grips, she no longer felt like she was on an ordinary bike—she felt like she was on a motorcycle.

A few minutes earlier when she whizzed by the house next door, Ronnie, the boy who lived there, shook his head and shouted, "Why are you riding a boy's bike?"

Evie snickered and replied, "Why do *you* play with Barbie's?"

Ronnie's eyes widened. "Do not!"

"Do too!"

And he did.

She'd seen him one day through her bedroom window.

Ronnie threw a stick, narrowly missing Evie's head. She thought about turning around, waving her middle finger in his direction. It was something she'd seen her grandmother do once when they were in the car together on the freeway. Evie decided against the gesture. Ronnie would just tell his mother, his mother would tell her grandmother, and she'd be in big trouble.

No crybaby was worth that.

Besides, she had places to go.

Evie stuck her tongue out and cranked her foot down on the pedal just as Ronnie reached for a handful of gravel. He hurled the small rocks into the air, aiming for her head, but his pitch was weak. Nothing hit her. Not a single one.

Crisis averted, Evie reached the park and rolled to a stop. She hopped off the bike, leaning it against a sawed-off trunk of a tree. She was debating whether it would be safe to leave it there when she heard a sound. Someone was crying. She climbed the grassy hillside to investigate. In the sand in front of the swings, she saw a girl who looked to be about her same age. The girl was on her knees, and she wasn't just crying—she was out-and-out bawling. Two boys hovered over the girl. One of them was taunting her, laughing; the other, awkward and still. The boys looked older by maybe a year or two. Given she could only see the backs of their heads, it was too hard to tell for sure.

She needed to get closer, check things out.

"What's the matter, little girl?" one of the boys teased. "Did someone take your swing away?"

"My name's not 'little girl.' It's Quinn, and you pushed me!"

"It's *our* turn on the swings," the same boy said. "Besides, what are *you* going do about it?"

From the looks of it, nothing.

Evie waited, giving Quinn a full minute to buck up and defend herself. But the girl remained where she was, staring at the ground.

"Hey!" Evie yelled. "Maybe *she's* not gonna do something about it, but I will."

The boy responsible for the taunting roared with laughter until he turned around and saw Evie standing in front of them, one of her fists raised in front of his face.

The other boy said, "Evie? What are you doing here?"

Evie looked at Quinn, noticing a tear in the knee of her thick, light-blue stockings and the sand scattered throughout her long, dark pigtails. Then she looked at the boy who'd recognized her. "Roman Tanner, say you're sorry!"

"He's not gonna do that," the other boy said. "We've been waiting for our turn on the swings forever. We asked her to get off the swing, and she ignored us. So, we ... well, helped her off of it."

Roman stood still, his eyes never leaving Evie as he said, "Dylan, maybe we should tell the girl we're sorry for what happened and—"

"You kiddin' me?" Dylan said. "No way. Don't let a *girl* tell you what to do."

Evie had heard enough.

She drilled her fist straight forward. It connected with Dylan's nose, and blood splashed out everywhere.

Quinn gasped.

Roman froze.

Evie smiled.

"Did you see what she did to me?!" Dylan cried.

Evie turned her attention to Roman. "Say you're sorry. Do it!"

Roman raised his hands. "All right, all right. I'm sorry!"

"Don't say it to me, you idiot," Evie said. "Say it to *her*."

Roman rolled his eyes and looked at Quinn. "Hey, I'm sorry. We didn't mean to hurt you, okay? Dylan should have never pushed you off the swing. We didn't know you'd get hurt. Honest."

"Good," Evie said. "Now get out of here, both of you."

The boys turned and went, Dylan shooting Evie a look like she may have gotten her way this time, but it was far from over. Evie didn't care. Grandma Ruby always told her bullies were the biggest wimps of them all, and looking at the tears trailing down Dylan's cheeks, she believed her.

Evie held out a hand.

Quinn took it and stood up.

"Wow," Quinn said. "They're scared of you."

"Not me, my Grandma Ruby. She's friends with Roman's grandma. He knows what would happen if I told her what he did. I wouldn't, though. I'm no squealer, and I've learned how to take care of myself. You should too."

Quinn shrugged. "Yeah, I guess so."

But Evie knew Quinn wasn't the type of girl to defend herself. One look at Quinn's dress and matching hair bows, and Evie knew everything she needed to know about her. Quinn was soft, easy, the perfect kind of girl bullies liked to tease. And she was thin, a lightweight. Evie imagined if she jabbed her with a pinkie finger she'd tip right over.

"Why haven't I seen you before?" Evie asked.

"We just moved here a couple weeks ago."

"Who's *we*?"

"My mom, dad, and my sister."

"Younger or older?" Evie asked.

"What?"

"Your sister. Is she younger or older?"

"Younger." Quinn rolled her eyes. "She's a pain. Follows me around everywhere."

Evie smiled.

Maybe Quinn *wasn't* so sweet after all.

"I'm Evie. What grade are you going into this year?"

"Fifth."

"Me too. Who's your teacher?"

"Mr. Landers."

"Hey, mine too." Quinn may have dressed a little too girly for Evie's tastes, but Evie admired the chain she wore around her neck. It was silver with two hearts interlocked around each other. "Cool necklace, by the way."

Quinn reached behind her neck, unclasped the necklace, and held it out to Evie. "It's yours."

"Oh, hey ... you don't have to give it to me just because I like it."

Quinn dropped the necklace into Evie's hands. "It's okay. I want you to have it. Wanna be friends?"

Evie nodded. "Sure, why not? Have you met anyone else since you moved here?"

"No, why?"

"If you want, you can hang out with me this year at school."

Quinn shrugged. "Okay."

"Good, it's settled then."

In the distance, Evie heard someone calling Quinn's name.

"That's my mom," Quinn said. "I have to go. See you around, okay?"

"Yeah, see you around. And hey, don't worry about those boys bothering you again. Roman's not so bad when he's not palling around with losers. Besides, when you're with me, I won't ever let anything bad happen to you."

2

F*ifteen Years Later*

Quinn Montgomery woke to the kind of blank darkness that left her feeling like she'd been tangled inside a web, suffocating for a good part of her adult life. Only she wasn't awake. She was swimming inside a dream, but none of her dreams had ever been this unsettling before.

Sounds bounced in and out of her consciousness—echoing and swirling like they were being broadcasted inside her mind through an elongated tunnel.

"Quinn, I need you to listen to me, to hear my voice," her father said. "Wake up for us, please. Open your eyes."

She tried opening her eyes, but she couldn't.

Where was he?

Or even more important—where was *she*?

And why wouldn't her eyes open?

"Come on, sweetheart," her father prompted. "Come back to us."

She tried again.

Still nothing.

A mixture of odors, pungent and sharp, penetrated her nostrils as she breathed in a lungful of sterile air. The smell was like a cloth had been doused in vinegar and slathered all over the room ... if, in fact, she was in a room. The fetid odor was soon replaced by another sensation—pressure, someone clutching her hand, squeezing so hard it felt like one of her knuckles had cracked.

"Quinn, can you hear me?" her mother asked. "We're right here with you, honey."

Her mother's voice sounded frail and thin and something else ... *scared*.

Someone placed a hand on her forehead, combing their fingers through her long, coffee-colored curls.

"She's not responding to us," her father said. "Why don't *you* give it a try?"

"I ... I don't know," came the response. "I wouldn't know what to say."

The newest voice Quinn heard was an unwelcome one—Marcus, her husband.

As thoughts raced through her mind, memories began to return, even though most of what had happened over the past twenty-four hours was still a blur.

"I don't think it matters what you say," her father said. "Quinn needs to know you're here, that you support her."

Quinn wanted to laugh out loud.

Support.

She doubted Marcus understood the meaning of the word.

"Talk to her like you would if she was awake," her father added. "That's all you need to do."

"If she was awake, she wouldn't talk to me," Marcus said. "Not after I—"

"You're her husband," her father cut in. "The past doesn't matter. Right now, Quinn needs all of us."

Thick, calloused fingers wound around her bony arm, and she cringed. She knew those fingers all too well. It felt like he'd moved closer to her, his breath steamy and hot as he whispered something into her ear.

"Quinn, it's Marcus. I'm here with your mom and your dad, and we all just want you to wake up, to come back to us. I'm sorry about Evie."

Evie.

In an instant, Quinn's fragmented memories flooded her mind, and she remembered everything—what had happened, where she was, and how she got here.

Evie was dead.

The night before, she'd received the horrible news about the tragic loss over the phone. At the time, Marcus had been yelling at her, just like he did almost every night, and in that moment, she'd realized something. She couldn't take one more second of living a life she'd wanted to run away from for years.

She had to get away—away from him.

Struggling to catch her breath after the phone call ended, she'd grabbed the car keys out of the bowl on the kitchen counter and sprinted from the house to her car, peeling out of the driveway. As she tore up the hill, her tires spitting fragments of freshly laid asphalt back onto the street, her eyes flooded with tears. She tried wiping them away but couldn't keep up. In the moments that followed, she lost control of the steering wheel, her car veering off the road, careening into a knotty, old tree. The last thing she remembered was a woman hovering over her, asking someone to call 9-1-1.

Now she rested on a hospital bed, her body bruised, heart broken.

Desperate pleas emitted from her mother's mouth, but they were overshadowed by something else. A sound, long and steady. A beeping that refused to end.

A male voice barked commands: "I need everyone to clear the room. Now!"

In a strange, twist of surreal reality, Quinn felt herself detach from her physical body, hovering between this life and the next. Time had spilled from the hourglass until all that remained were a few tiny grains.

Part of her wanted to live, to fight, to make something more of her life.

The other part was tired and broken and didn't want to wake to a world if Evie wasn't in it.

3

T*wo Days Later*

The last time Quinn had seen Evie, Evie asked if she was happy, as she'd done many times in the past year. Not wanting her friend to worry, Quinn had assured her everything was fine, even though it wasn't.

At present, Marcus was standing across from her hospital bed, leaning against the wall. Quinn had just asked him to leave, and based on his expression, he wasn't keen on the idea.

"You almost died, Quinn," he said. "I don't think you should be alone right now."

"I'm fine," Quinn said. "I feel a lot better today. I'm going to talk to the doctor when he stops by and ask him when I can get out of here."

"You can't *leave*. You're still recovering from the accident."

It was just like him to say those words.

He was always trying to make decisions for her, and today was no different.

Dressed in single-cuff, black trousers, striped socks, and new, polished loafers, Marcus was no longer the board-shorts-wearing surfer he used to be, and Quinn wondered where that man had gone. When they first met, he was charming and flirty. The man standing before her now was so different, he was almost unrecognizable.

She attempted to slide off the hospital bed and stand, but her wobbly legs disapproved. She reached out, wrapping a hand around the bed railing, doing what she could to steady herself while Marcus looked on, his arms folded, head shaking, disapproving.

Always disapproving.

"I talked to the nurse earlier about being released," Quinn said. "She thinks the doctor will sign off on it if I have people to look after me when I leave here, and I do. If he allows it, I'll have a few forms to fill out, and then I'm free to go."

"Where's the doctor? I want to talk to him."

"Please, Marcus. Don't make a big deal out of it, okay?"

"It *is* a big deal. If this guy thinks it's all right to release you this soon, maybe we need to get a second opinion, because I don't agree with it."

His temper was flaring, and she hadn't even delivered the worst news yet.

"Since you're here, there's something else we need to talk about," she said.

"Oh, yeah? What's that?"

"My parents will be going home tomorrow morning," she said. "If the doctor discharges me, I've decided to go with them to Cody."

"Wyoming isn't *home*, Quinn. Not anymore. Your home is here with me, the same place it's been for the last six years."

But was Utah *her* home?

Or was it his?

Marcus stomped a foot onto the floor. "Come on, now. Be realistic. Get back into bed. You need rest."

She shook her head. "I'm going back to Cody, Wyoming. I want to be there for Evie's funeral."

He stepped forward, jabbing a finger in front of her face. "You're in no condition to go anywhere, and you know it."

Two days ago, his comment would have signaled the end of a discussion in which the old, timid Quinn would have given in. Over the years she'd learned relenting was a lot easier than fighting for herself. But now, a more determined Quinn was emerging, and this new woman's eyes were wide open.

"I've already made my decision," she said. "I'm going home with my parents."

"I don't understand what's happening right now. You're ... you're not yourself."

"You're wrong. I'm feel more like myself than I have in a long time."

"I'm your husband. I know you, and your actions, your behaviors ... This," he swirled a finger in the air, "what's happening right now, it isn't you. Bottom line is, I don't want you to go, and as your husband, I have a say in the matter."

They squared off, Quinn staring at Marcus, Marcus staring back.

As a husband, Marcus had always been faithful. He was reliable, and he had a great job. But the longer they were married, the more she saw him for who he truly was—a bully. As days rolled into years, she recognized herself less and less, until the little bit of light remaining in her soul had been snuffed out.

A nurse popped her head inside the hospital room, smiling at Quinn as she said, "Hey, hun. Just checking on you. Is there anything you need?"

"I'm fine, thank you," Quinn said.

"The cafeteria is open. If there's anything you'd like me to get for—"

"She said she's fine," Marcus cut in. "If she needs something from the cafeteria. Not that the food in this place is edible, because it isn't."

The nurse narrowed her eyes at him as she stood in the doorway. Then she glanced at Quinn, waiting until she'd nodded before the nurse backed into the hallway, leaving the door open a crack.

Marcus leaned to the side as if looking to see if the nurse was still within earshot. Then he shifted his focus back to Quinn. "All right. I'll tell you what ... if you're released, I'll agree to take you to Wyoming. We'll both attend the funeral so you can have the closure you need, and then we'll come back here. All I want is for things to get back to normal again."

Normal.

She didn't even know what normal was anymore.

All she knew was the time had come to have an even more difficult conversation, one Marcus wouldn't want to hear. She'd thought about waiting until they were back at home, but she'd spent enough of her life waiting, living her life for someone else.

Evie would want her to stand up for herself.

It was time.

"Marcus, I've done a lot of thinking over the last two days," Quinn said.

"Oh, yeah? About what?"

"About our marriage and our life together."

He raised a brow. "And?"

"I'm not right for you, and you're not right for me. I don't think we ever were."

He responded with a simple shrug of his shoulders,

unfazed, acting as if she hadn't said much of anything at all. "That's the meds talking. You don't mean it."

"You haven't touched me, *really* touched me, in a long time. I can't even remember the last time we were … the last time we had sex. I bet you don't know either. That's how long it's been."

He rubbed his hands together, huffing out a frustrated, "It's just something we're going through, something all marriages go through."

"No, it isn't. It's more than that."

"Where's this coming from?"

"I want to find purpose and meaning in my life again, and I want to stop holding on to the past. Our son has been dead for two years. We weren't doing great before he died, and since then … well, it's gotten even worse. I'm not happy, and if you're being honest with yourself, neither are you."

Marcus reached out, tracing a finger up and down her arm. "I love you, but I don't know how much more of this nonsense I can take."

"I'm sorry. I know this isn't what you want to hear, but I meant what I said. I *am* leaving with my parents tomorrow."

"So you've said, over and over again. If I wanted a constant repeat, I'd buy a parrot. Like I said before, *I'll* drive you. There's no need to hitch a ride with your parents."

Quinn took a deep breath in, gripping the bed sheet in her hand as she whispered, "I didn't want to have this conversation here, but since we are, I want to be honest with you. I'm not just going to Cody for Evie's funeral. I'm leaving here, for good."

He moved a hand to his hip. "What are you talking about?"

She paused a moment, taking in a deep breath as she gathered the courage to say what she needed to next. "I'm leaving our marriage."

He went silent for a moment, and then he bent toward her, gritting his teeth as he said, "Are you out of your mind?"

He fisted a hand, and Quinn waited for him to hit some-thing, what he often did when he was angry. But he didn't. He stood there—stunned.

"I'm sorry to tell you like this, Marcus," Quinn said. "Truly, I am."

"Don't be."

"I'm not saying any of this to hurt you."

"Oh, don't worry," he scoffed. "You haven't."

He blew past her, and she closed her eyes, listening to the high-pitched squeak of the rubber on the bottom of his shoes as they advanced down the hall.

Away from her.

Away from their life together.

The veil of darkness had been lifted at long last.

She reopened her eyes, and for the first time in a long time, she breathed in a full, cleansing breath—a breath that was the start of a new beginning.

4

Eighteen medium-sized boxes. It was hard to believe a few handfuls of cardboard was all Quinn's life had amounted to after so many years. She pondered the thought as she peeled a piece of packing tape from the dispenser and onto the last box.

At the age of twenty-six, it was hard to believe she was moving back in with her parents again. Sure, she'd be in a separate casita behind the main house, but who was she kidding? It was like she was experiencing life in reverse.

Quinn stacked the box she was holding on top of another and turned, smoothing a hand over a box her mother had labeled "Isaiah" in black marker. The name had been scribbled inside a heart. Tracing the image with her finger, she reminded herself that Isaiah was no longer alone in the afterlife—Evie would find him.

In many ways, starting over again made her feel like she was going into the next chapter of her journey empty-handed. Her book of life seemed closed, the pages stuck together and unable to be turned. She had no idea what the future held, but she knew one thing—leaving Marcus had been the right decision.

Quinn's father entered the room, placing a supportive hand on her shoulder. At six foot four, he towered over her five-foot-eight frame. He was in his early sixties, and his hair had started going gray, but he still looked as fit as he'd ever been. A devout vegetarian with a workout regimen that included jogging five miles each morning, it wasn't hard to see why he'd held up so well. Or why he was the perfect match for her mother, a woman with a cocoa-colored pixie cut and the looks of a modern-day Grace Kelly.

"I'm surprised Marcus isn't here to say goodbye," her father said.

"He won't be here, Dad. He doesn't want to see me right now. He might not ever want to see me again after our conversation yesterday. And the truth is, I don't blame him. The decision I made was the right one for both of us. Still feels lousy though."

Since announcing her decision to divorce to her parents, her mother had spent a fair amount of time humming. Although she'd always kept her feelings about Marcus to herself, Quinn knew her mother had never felt he was the right man for her. Hence the humming—and the permanent smile affixed to her face.

Her father crossed the room, uttering something in her mother's ear. It was too low for Quinn to hear. They glanced in her direction and then hushed their voices again.

Her mother was no longer smiling.

"What's going on with you two?" Quinn asked. "If you're worried about me because of all that's happened over the last couple of days, I'll be all right. It will take some time, but one of these days soon, I'll pull myself together."

"Quinn, why don't we all take five and sit down for a

minute?" her father suggested. "There's something we need to talk to you about."

A cool tingling sensation trailed up her arms. She didn't know why, only that the somber looks on their faces were cause for concern.

Her friend was dead.

Her marriage was dead.

How much worse could it get?

Tears began to trail down her mother's face, and her father reached out, draping an arm around his wife. "If this is too hard for you, Jane, I can have this discussion with Quinn myself."

Her mother shook her head. "Evie was like a daughter to me, Mitchell. She was like a daughter to both of us. I want to stay. Quinn deserves to know the truth."

What *truth*?

"Dad?" Quinn asked. "What's going on?"

"When I called and told you Evie had passed away," her father began, "I suppose I ... I didn't tell you everything. We wanted to see you first, talk to you in person, you see."

"Talk to me in person about what?"

Her parents exchanged worried glances.

"I'd discussed it with your mother beforehand, and we decided it was best to wait until we had more information about Evie's death before sharing the details with you. Then we received the call from Marcus letting us know you were in the hospital. We got in the car and drove straight here ... and, well, you know the rest."

Quinn looked at her parents and decided maybe her father's suggestion to sit down a minute ago was the right one. She took a seat, staring up at him and saying, "What is it? What do you need to tell me?"

"Before, when we spoke on the phone, I told you Evie's death was an accident. The police hadn't released a lot of information yet, so we were all speculating as to what happened." He cleared his throat once, then a second time. "There's no easy way to say this, Quinn. I wish there was, but there isn't. From what we've been told, Evie's death wasn't an accident."

"I don't understand. How can you be sure? If it wasn't an accident, what happened?"

"We spoke with one of our neighbors this morning. And ... well, the neighbor told us the police have now confirmed foul play was involved. Honey, Evie was murdered."

5

Bo McAllister blinked a few times before convincing himself what he was seeing was real. Quinn Montgomery was sitting two rows in front of him, the closest they'd been to each other since she broke off their relationship at the end of their senior year in high school. He knew she'd been in town over the years, visiting her family, meeting with old friends, and spending time with Evie. The small town of Cody was home to less than ten thousand residents, and yet she'd managed to evade him every single time until today.

Sometimes he wondered if it was on purpose.

Other times he was sure of it.

Seeing her again, his stomach festered with a sick, uncomfortable queasiness. He'd thought of her often throughout the years, hoping one day he'd get a chance to clear the air, to resolve the one thing she'd never allowed him to explain, and perhaps give her the opportunity to do the same. Part of him still resented her for ending the relationship the way she had. Another part longed to be in her presence again. Now here she was, dressed in a fitted black dress with capped sleeves, looking fragile and pale, and in pain.

It wasn't the kind of reunion he'd imagined.

Not with Evie gone.

Despite the gap in time, Quinn had aged like a fine wine. Sophisticated and well preserved, with the same dark, lustrous dark hair he remembered. The same long, thin neck and defined collarbone that set her apart from every other woman in a crowd. Different eyes, though, but it was obvious she'd been crying. He remembered her eyes changed on occasion, much like the colors in a mood ring. Today the bright orbs of jade had turned a hazy shade of gray.

And why wouldn't they?

She was grieving.

Evie had been more like a sister to Quinn than a friend. He assumed the news of her murder had come as a shock, as it should have. Murders weren't common in Cody. The entire town was reeling over it.

When Quinn had entered the funeral home an hour earlier, he'd observed a nasty two-inch gash over her right eye and bruising on her arms and legs. They looked fresh, and he wondered how the injuries had happened.

Had it been an accident?

Or was it the result of something else ... something more sinister?

Earlier, their eyes had met, and he'd raised a hand, trying to get her attention. She seemed to discount the gesture, acting like she hadn't seen him, even though he was certain she had. He wasn't surprised. She could hold a grudge longer than any woman he'd ever known. Seven years, and he just knew she still wasn't over what had happened.

Bo's attention switched from Quinn to Jacob, Evie's four-year-old son. The boy slid off his father's knee, his arms outstretched toward Quinn. She waved him over, pulling him onto her lap, wrapping her slender arms around him. Jacob leaned against her, his eyes fluttering open and closed as she rested her cheek on the side of his head, stroking his fine tufts of blond hair while she rocked him. She lulled him to sleep for a short time before his eyes shot open, a look of fear and panic covering his face. He stared at Quinn and then buried his head in her chest, locking his arms around her neck.

Quinn stood, a tear trailing down her cheek as she cradled Jacob in her arms, carrying him to the back of the room. She glanced in Bo's direction for a split second when she passed and then her eyes darted away again.

Bo had been so caught up in Quinn's presence he hadn't noticed the minister was no longer standing at the pulpit. Ruby, Evie's grandmother, had taken his place—a spirited woman in her eighties with a vehement personality that rivaled every old-timer in town.

By the looks of things, Ruby's talk was nearing the end, an end that sent a wave of horrific gasps throughout the room when Ruby shaped her frail hand into a pistol, aiming it at the crowd.

Eyes wide, she waved the finger gun around, saying, "I intend to find the person responsible for robbing me of my final years with my granddaughter. And when I do, no judge or jury will decide his fate. I'll personally see to it that he *or* she is sent straight to hell!"

6

Quinn sat on a bench at the back of the room, waiting for everyone to shuffle out of the funeral home. She hoped to get one final farewell before Evie's body was carted off to its final resting place. But who was she kidding? Evie's body have been in the same room as Quinn, but Evie's spirit was long gone. Quinn could say whatever she liked to Evie in the casket. She could yell if she wanted. She could scream. None of it would make the slightest difference.

It wasn't Evie.

Still, Quinn walked to the front of the room, hunching over as she pressed her hands onto the lid of the casket. It almost felt like she was at a funeral for someone else, like it wasn't real.

"I miss you, Evie," she said. "I have no idea how to be in this life without you. I don't know what to do now that you're gone. You've been my strength for so long, I suppose I never learned to find strength in myself. I know I have to now. It's what you would want, even though all I want is to see your face again, to speak to you one last time, to tell you how much I—"

She heard a rustling sound and turned, her eyes coming to

rest on Bo. He was standing at the back of the room, staring at her, his expression one of concern.

Was his worry for her?

Had he heard what she'd just said?

She didn't know, and she was far too caught up in her emotions to care.

They stared at each other for a long moment, and she waited for him to approach, but he didn't. He tipped his head toward her, saying nothing as he ducked out of the room. Quinn stood motionless for a time, her thoughts turning to the past—a past she'd tried to forget, even though it lingered.

This isn't the time or the place.

Today is about Evie.

Willing herself back into the present, she faced the casket once more. The decision not to leave it open had been the right one. As the details of Evie's murder had started to emerge, Quinn learned her friend had been murdered at home while soaking in the bathtub. She'd been shot twice—once in the chest and once in the head—her murderer taking every precaution to ensure she was dead.

He was a butcher.

A coward.

A cold-blooded killer willing to gun Evie down while her child was present in the home.

Who would do such a thing?

And why?

As the tears began to flow, she threw herself over the coffin, an unspeakable void coming over her as the beginnings of an unquenchable need started to build.

A feeling of rage, and a need ... a need for revenge.

7

A drab mixture of colors swelled across a grumbling sky. It was like the heavens had dipped a finger into a vat of black ink and another into gray, painting a canvas fit for a somber afternoon. Quinn stood, arms crossed in front of her, staring out Ruby's living room window.

At present, Ruby's house was crowded with people who'd gathered to pay their respects. And while Quinn appreciated their gestures of kindness, she found herself eyeing the front door. She wondered if anyone would attempt to engage her in conversation if she crossed the room and dipped outside for some fresh air. It wasn't that she wanted to avoid engaging with those in attendance. She knew she couldn't, not without her emotions getting the best of her. So she played it safe and remained in place, sipping on chamomile tea and recalling memories of her and Evie, playing in the same front yard she was staring at now.

If she concentrated hard enough, she could almost turn back the hands of time, visualizing the two of them together, talking and laughing, as if it were happening in this very moment. It was the little things, the things taken for granted that she'd miss the most, like the way Evie giggled with her mouth closed when she thought something was funny.

Ever since Quinn's arrival, Ruby was nowhere to be found. One of Evie's cousins was overheard saying Ruby had been "drugged up," perhaps given a Xanax or something even stronger to help her relax.

A hand trailed down Quinn's back and she turned, relieved to see her mother standing in front of her.

"You look pale," her mother said. "How are you feeling? Can I get you something to eat?"

Quinn shook her head. "I tried one of the casseroles someone brought. It was delicious, but my stomach isn't doing so good, and I'm having a hard time being here. I feel like I'm a mess, Mom, like my entire world is falling apart all around me."

"This is just how you're feeling right now, sweetheart. It's normal given all that's happened in the past week. You've experienced a shock and a huge loss. It will take time to heal. The best thing you can do right now is to be gentle with yourself."

"Have you seen Ruby?"

"I have. She's in her room."

"How's she doing?"

"Better than she was earlier, though I suppose it's still difficult for her to accept what's happened."

After a falling out with her daughter, Peggy, several years before, Ruby discovered Peggy had born a child, a girl she named Evangeline, 'Evie' for short. The child had been living in foster care. Unable to care for her daughter, Peggy had taken her to the neighbor's house one morning, promising she'd "be back within the hour."

An entire day passed before the neighbor accepted the inevitable truth.

Peggy was gone for good.

She wasn't returning for her daughter.

The neighbor made a call, and child services intervened. Ruby was located, and she wasted no time filing a petition with the state to gain custody of her granddaughter, which she was awarded. Just as the neighbor had suspected, Peggy never returned, making Ruby the only mother Evie had ever known. Not only had Ruby just lost her granddaughter, she'd lost a daughter as well.

As Quinn pondered that fact, she glanced across the room, her eyes darting back and forth between Bo and her father, who were engaged in conversation.

Bo looked good, considering how much time had passed since she saw him last. Now he sported a trimmed goatee. His thick hair was still worn the same way as it had always been, off his forehead and parted to the side. A few rebellious hairs strayed from the rest, out of place, giving him the appearance of a reddish-brown-haired Tom Hardy, only younger and several inches taller.

Bo glanced at Quinn and smiled, showing off what Quinn had always considered to be his most attractive features—his wide, full lips and his dimples. She'd been so caught up stealing glances at him over the past several minutes, a finger tap on her shoulder caught her off guard, and she jumped.

"I'm sorry," the man said. "I didn't mean to startle you."

"Oh, hey, Roman. I didn't see you there. How are you?"

He tipped the beer bottle he was holding to his lips and took a long swig. "I don't know, if I'm being honest. Numb, I guess. You?"

Shattered into a million pieces, although she couldn't bring herself to say it.

"I don't know how I am right now either," she said.

"I don't think anyone who cared about Evie does. We're all in shock." He lifted a finger, pointing at the bruises on her arm. "Hey ... are you, ahh, okay? You're kinda banged up."

"I was in a car accident. I'm fine. I'm still ..."

Alive was what she meant to say, but she stopped herself.

Quinn waited for him to say something more, but he just stood there, blinking at her.

Roman was Evie's ex-husband, and he'd always been a man of few words, though today, it was obvious even simple chitchat was a strain. Still, he'd tapped *her* on the shoulder, causing her to wonder if there was something he intended to say.

"Is there anything you'd like to talk to me about?" Quinn asked.

"I ... uhh, yeah. I guess so."

Another pause.

She placed a hand on his shoulder. "It's all right. I'm finding it hard to talk to anyone today too."

"He was supposed to be with me that night."

"Who was supposed to be with you—Jacob?"

Roman nodded. "It was my turn to have him, but one of my employees didn't show up for work, so I had to cover for him."

"It's not your fault. You couldn't have known. None of us could have."

"I ... I want you to know, I didn't do it."

"Didn't do *what*?"

"I don't know what happened to Evie, or why, but I'd never do anything to hurt her."

Roman's startling non-confession caught her off guard. "I never said you did anything to hurt her."

"I know *you* haven't."

His emphasis on the word *you* incited a curious reaction from the room, one she hadn't noticed before. Others in the vicinity were eyeing Roman, and not everyone was looking at him in a positive way.

"Has someone suspected you of being involved with Evie's death?" Quinn asked. "If they have, that's ridiculous."

He shrugged. "Cops keep coming around, asking questions. Wasn't sure whether you knew that or not. I'm working with them, though. Working together, you might say."

"I'm sure they're talking to everyone right now. It doesn't mean you're a suspect. It's protocol, the same rigmarole they're obligated to do with everyone. I bet they'll want to talk to me too."

"It's more than that, Quinn. They showed up at my house with a warrant. Didn't find anything. I told them they wouldn't. There's nothing to find."

"Give it time. I bet they ease off."

Roman ran an unsteady hand down the side of his shaggy, thick mane of hair, and he leaned in closer.

"Whatever anyone tells you, and no matter what happens, it's important you hear the truth from my own lips," he said. "Evie's death was someone else's doing. Understand?"

What alarmed Quinn the most wasn't the stern look on Roman's face, the fact he'd encroached on her personal space, or his sincere plea for her approval. For everything he'd just said, she got the feeling there *was* something he was withholding, something he was unwilling to say.

"Roman, I meant what I said before," she said. "I don't believe you'd ever harm Evie."

As if realizing how close he was to her, he took a step back and nodded, breathing a sigh of relief.

She considered reaching out and pulling him into an embrace. He looked like he needed one. But he'd always shied away from public affection when he was married to Evie, so she decided the best thing she could do was to give him some space.

Roman shoved his hands into his vest pockets. A plastic pill bottle tumbled out, landing on Ruby's thick, mauve carpet. He reached down, snatched the bottle in his shaking hand, removed the lid, and popped two pills in his mouth. Then he shoved the bottle back inside his pocket.

Quinn wondered what the pills were, but she didn't dare ask.

"Thanks for taking Jacob earlier, during the funeral," he said. "It means a lot."

"Anytime. He's like a son to me."

"I do my best with him, you know? But I'm not sure how I'll ever fill Evie's shoes."

Roman may not have been a man Quinn considered to be excellent father material, but she never doubted his love for Jacob. He just lacked the skills needed to express his feelings sometimes.

While Roman had excelled at everything—from all-state in high school basketball to owning the most popular bar in town—bonding with others had never come easy for him. Quinn thought back to when Evie and Roman first started dating. Evie had been so optimistic. Never one to back down from a challenge, she discovered that Roman was the biggest one of all. Evie was convinced she was the one woman who could relate to Roman's closed-off nature, the one woman who could fix him, get him to open up. But he never did, not in the way she'd needed. After a while, their marriage became strained, and when Evie couldn't justify staying any longer, she filed for divorce.

"I think what matters most is letting Jacob know you're here for him right now," Quinn said. "If you need me, for anything, just ask. I'm not going anywhere."

He paused then said, "Jacob seems to be doing a lot better now that you're here. I was wondering how you would feel ... if he could, ahh, stay with you tonight?"

"Hasn't he been staying with Ruby the last couple of nights?"

"Yeah, it's just—"

"You don't have to explain. I saw what happened today. Everyone did. It might be good for Ruby to have some time to herself."

"What's bugging me is something other than the tantrum she threw at the viewing," he said. "I'm not comfortable with what's happening when Ruby's with Jacob."

"I'm not sure I understand what you mean."

"Ruby's been trying to get Jacob to tell her what happened. You know he was in the house with Evie the night she died, right?"

"I do. My father told me."

Roman paused a moment, then leaned in close. "What most people don't know is, Jacob isn't talking, *period*. Hasn't said a single word to anyone, not since Evie was murdered."

8

Quinn hovered in the doorway of one of the casita's bedrooms, watching Jacob's chest rise and fall. Every few minutes, he sucked rapid gasps of air through his lungs like he was trapped in a bad dream. After rocking him for a solid hour earlier, he'd finally succumbed to sleep.

As she kept a watchful eye on him, questions ran wild inside her mind.

Had Evie known someone wanted her dead?

What had Jacob seen the night Evie died?

Did Evie *know* her attacker?

Did Jacob?

Why had she been murdered?

And the biggest query of them all—if the killer wasn't caught, would the murders continue? Or had Evie's death been personal, a single, premeditated attack?

Jacob had been left unharmed, another oddity.

Perhaps the boy had hidden, and the killer never even knew he was there.

Or perhaps the killer was aware of Jacob's presence, and

he'd taken compassion on him, sparing him the same fate his mother endured.

With exception to a few unusual incidents over the years, the town of Cody had always been considered a happy, restful place, safe and protected from the outside world as if it were inside its own impenetrable bubble. People left their front doors unlocked, keys inside the ignitions of their vehicles. Some people even kept their vehicles running in winter while they shopped at one of the local stores.

Now things had changed, residents were on high alert. Quinn could see it in their faces. Not fear. Fear was for sissies. Fear didn't exist in the rugged, tough-as-nails state of Wyoming. It was something else—a deep-rooted, vengeful indignation. The man responsible for Evie's death had messed with the wrong town and the wrong kind of people—a big mistake.

In Cody, a town named after one of its founders, William Frederick Cody, also known as Buffalo Bill, townspeople banded together. The sound of firearms being prepped reverberated a fierce warning from one corner of town to the other. Maybe it wouldn't be today, and maybe it wouldn't be tomorrow, but sometime in the not-too-distant future, a valuable lesson would be learned: screw with Wyoming, and Wyoming screws right back.

A light rapping at the door jarred Quinn away from her thoughts. She glanced at the time. It was late, after eleven o'clock. She tiptoed down the hallway and eased the door open, trying her best to keep quiet.

Bo poked his head inside. "Hey, I know it's been a while, and I'm sorry it's so late. I was hoping we could chat for a minute. I have a few things I'd like to—"

"I'm sorry ... I can't talk right now. It's not a good time."

He glanced past her. "Why not? Is your husband here? I didn't see anyone with you earlier, or at the wake."

"He's not my ... I'm not ... I don't want to talk about ..."

Less complicated, Quinn.

Less complicated.

"He's not here," she said.

"Look, I know how things ended with us, and maybe you're still angry about the whole thing. I get it. It's just ... ever since I saw you at the funeral, you've been on my mind. I came to see how you were holding up. If we can't talk now, when can we?"

"I don't know. Later. Not *tonight* later. *Later, later.*"

Bo pressed a hand to his lips, suppressing a laugh. "How *much* later is *later* later?"

Quinn threw her hands in the air. "I don't know. I have a lot going on right now."

"Are you making excuses because you don't want to talk to me?"

"It has nothing to do with you ... or me, for that matter."

"Then why can't we talk now?"

Down the hall, Quinn heard the one sound she was hoping to avoid—Jacob's tender, panicked voice exploding through the air, "Winn! Winn!"

Quinn closed her eyes, breathing out a long, frustrated sigh.

Unable to say the name Quinn, "Winn" was the name Jacob always called her.

As if realizing why it wasn't a good time for Quinn to talk, Bo hung his head. "I didn't ... I'm so sorry, Quinn. I had no idea you had Jacob tonight, or I never would have come."

Quinn swung around, saying nothing as she started down the hall toward the child. "I'm here, and I'm coming, sweetie."

She entered the bedroom and found Jacob sitting up in bed, sniffling. She bent down, pulling him into her arms. "It's okay, sweetheart. I'm right here. Everything's all right. I've got you."

Jacob curled his hand around Quinn's fingers, staring up at her as he said, "Bad dream, bad person. Don't leave, Winn."

"I won't. I'm here now. You don't need to worry. Okay?"

Bo stepped into the room, pressing a hand to his mouth for a moment. Then he said "I can't believe it."

"Can't believe *what*?" Quinn snapped.

"He's talking again."

9

Roman Chapman sat on the edge of a mattress that rested atop a handcrafted, four-poster bed. He smoothed the tips of his fingers over the side of one of the knotty wood posts, reflecting on the countless hours he'd spent on its creation. After seeing the gleam in Evie's eye when she fawned over a similar bed in a department store window, he'd purchased the wood at the local lumberyard and carved an almost identical bed by hand.

The unique piece of furniture had been a gift to Evie on their wedding day. He'd even personalized it, etching "R + E" on the back of the headboard. Hidden from view, it had been sacred, only known to the two of them. For months after their split, he considering selling it, but no matter what the offer, when it was time for the deal to be done, he'd never been able to bring himself to do it. The bed was a part of him now, so much so he'd never part from it, not at any price.

Across the room, a five-by-seven photograph of Evie in her wedding dress had been stuck to the wall. She was all smiles, flashing a mouthful of sparkling whites for the person behind the camera. Staring at the photo made him recall a phone conversation they'd had months earlier. After several minutes of bickering, she'd hung up on him. Enraged, he'd swatted the picture frame harder than intended. It launched off the dresser, the glass shattering as it hit the floor. Still, he wasn't about to get rid of it. He'd tossed the frame and bits of glass in the trash, sticking the photo to the wall with a piece of tape.

Thinking about the night when everything had ignited—in a good way—between them, he tugged the photo free and ran his finger over a scratch where the glass has punctured the paper.

That night, she'd walked into his bar, plopped down on a barstool, and ordered a drink. A dry martini, extra olives. He'd made the drink and slid it over, watching as she swirled the olives around inside the glass.

Something was bothering her.

He could tell.

"Are you all right?" he'd asked.

She didn't look at him. She hadn't since she entered the bar.

"No, I'm not *all right.*"

"You remember me, don't you? We went to school together."

She glanced up, narrowing her eyes as she studied his face.

"Of course I remember you, Roman," she said. "Haven't seen you for a while."

"How have you been?"

She shook her head, said nothing.

"Do you want to talk about whatever is bothering you?" he asked.

"Not tonight. Hey, can I trouble you for a few more olives?"

He reached under the counter, unscrewed the lid on the olive jar, and placed it in front of her. "The olives are on the house. So's the advice."

"What advice?"

"Whoever he is, he doesn't deserve you."

"Him ... who?"

"Whoever caused you to come here tonight, alone."

For a moment, he thought he'd pushed her too far.

She spun the olive glass around, her eyes fixed on his.

Then she leaned back, shot him a wink, and said, "Touché."

And that was the beginning of everything.

Twenty-four hours later, they went out on their first date, spending most of the time reminiscing about how much they'd lost touch over the years. They talked about the day at the park when Quinn had been pushed off the swing, something Roman said he'd always regretted.

Nine months later, they married.

It seemed like a lifetime ago now.

Thinking back on the memories they'd shared, he realized being with Evie was the only time in his life he'd ever felt truly alive, and he was riddled with regret. There were so many things he would have done differently if he could step back in time with one last chance to do it all over again. He would have never let her go, never let her leave in the first place. Evie was the only person who had ever understood him, the only woman he'd ever loved. With her gone, he felt helpless, a ship without its anchor. But no matter how he felt, he needed to get it together for the sake of their son.

Roman glanced to the side, watching Buffy, Evie's cocker spaniel, poke the bedroom door open using the tip of her nose. She slid inside and hopped up on the bed next to him. She hadn't been her usual, playful self ever since he'd picked her up from Evie's house. He'd tossed her favorite green rubber ball down the hall a few times, knowing how she'd always loved to chase it. Now when he threw it, she sank to the ground, watching the bouncy ball skip and roll until it stopped.

"Come on, girl. Let's get you a bone. Whaddya say?"

She showed no interest, and Roman reached out, scooping her into his arms and carrying her to the kitchen. He grabbed a bone out of the pantry and headed back to his room. Setting Buffy beside him on the bed, he pressed the picture of Evie to his lips. Then he popped some sleeping pills into his mouth, washing them down with a hefty gulp of lager.

He'd never see his sweet love again, the only woman meant for him ... except maybe, if he was lucky, in his dreams.

10

It was twenty minutes past ten the following morning and Roman still hadn't arrived to pick up Jacob. Quinn wasn't alarmed. Evie always said his time management skills were lacking. No reason to expect a change in his routine now.

A text message popped up on Quinn's phone. It was from her mother, inviting her and Jacob to join them for breakfast. Since waking an hour earlier, he was back to not speaking again. Quinn wasn't alarmed about that, though. He was smiling, scribbling a rainbow of colors across a piece of paper. For now, he seemed content, and content was enough for her.

Quinn walked over to Jacob, squatting in front of him as she said, "Are you hungry, sweetheart?"

He nodded.

"Why don't we go get something to eat? You can finish your beautiful picture after breakfast. Sound good?"

Another nod.

Quinn took Jacob's hand, and together they walked to her parents' home. The screen door snapped closed when they entered, and she heard her mother's melodic voice say, "Quinn, is that you? Come see who's here."

She assumed her mother was referring to Roman, but when she entered the kitchen, she faced someone else, someone she hadn't seen in some time—her sister, Astrid.

"Hey, sis," Astrid said. "How are ya?"

Quinn feigned a smile. "Fine."

Astrid was sitting on the kitchen counter, her long, stringy, bleach-blond locks falling in loose curls over her body-hugging T-shirt. Standing in next to her was a man who looked to be pushing forty, making him almost twice her sister's age. Quinn wasn't surprised. It wasn't the first time Astrid had brought an older man home. She was a master at pushing their parents' buttons, and today was no exception.

"When did you get into town?" Quinn asked.

"Late last night."

"You missed Evie's funeral."

Astrid shrugged. "I know. Sorry. I thought about going. I've just never liked funerals. They creep me out ... and I wasn't sure you'd want me there."

If she hadn't come for the funeral, why was she here? Astrid didn't see family much, and when she did, it was often because she needed or wanted something.

"You haven't visited Mom and Dad for a long time," Quinn said. "It's been what ... a year or more?"

Astrid ignored the comment and shifted her attention to Jacob, stretching a stiff hand toward him. "Come over here and let me give you a squeeze, little one. I won't bite."

Jacob shook his head, ducking behind Quinn as and wrapping his arms around her leg.

"Why don't you let me take him for the day?" Astrid said. "That way, you can get some rest. You look like you need it."

"I don't. I'm fine. The bruises look worse than they feel."

"*Girls,*" Quinn's mother said. "Try to get along with each

other, okay? You're both a bit too old to be arguing, don't you think?"

"We weren't arguing," Astrid said. "We were talking."

The man standing beside Astrid cleared his throat and pushed a clammy hand toward Quinn. "The name's Eugene. Nice to meet you."

"Eugene owns half the car dealerships in the county," Astrid said.

It was then Quinn realized where she'd seen him before. It was on television, in his car commercials.

"Have you two been together long?" Quinn asked.

"Almost a month now," Eugene said.

"Let's eat," Quinn's mother suggested. "The food's getting cold."

Astrid hopped off the counter, and they all moved to the table.

"Where's Dad?" Quinn asked. "Has he gone out for a run?"

"No, I'm right here."

Quinn glanced up, detecting a hint of uneasiness in her father's voice when he entered the room. His face was rigid, almost haggard looking.

"Dad, is something wrong?" Quinn asked.

Turning toward her mother, he said, "Jane, why don't you dish up a plate for Jacob and take him over to the casita for few minutes?"

"But we just sat down, Mitchell."

Her parents exchanged glances, and her mother raised a brow, seeming to pick up on the nonverbal cue her father was giving. She put some bacon, eggs, and fruit on a plate and stood, reaching for Jacob's hand. "Come with me, sweetheart. Let's see what toys we can find, shall we?"

Jacob shook his head, refusing to move.

"Jacob," Quinn prompted, "I think I saw some chocolate

bars in the freezer over there. If you go with my mom, I bet she'll give you one when you finish your breakfast. I'll come over in a few minutes, okay? I'm not going anywhere. I promise."

He slid off the chair, bowed his head, and followed Quinn's mother out of the room.

Once he was out of earshot, Quinn faced her father. "What's happened? Do you have more news about Evie?"

"I just got off the phone with Bo," her father said.

The night before, when he'd stopped over and realized Jacob was staying the night, he'd given his apologies and left, telling Quinn he'd swing by another time.

Concerned about why he'd called her father, Quinn said, "I'd rather not talk about Bo right now."

"The phone call had nothing to do with you," her father said. "It concerns Roman."

"Roman was supposed to be here to pick up Jacob almost an hour ago."

"Evie never changed the beneficiary of her life insurance policy after the divorce," her father said. "Roman was to inherit half a million dollars."

Quinn wasn't surprised Evie hadn't changed the policy.

Evie had often been forgetful.

"I stopped by the grocery store this morning and ran into my friend Alicia," Astrid said. "You know, people in town think Roman murdered Evie."

Quinn spun around, narrowing her eyes at her sister. "What *people*?"

"Alicia said the cops have evidence."

"What *evidence*? And how would Alicia know?"

"A shoe print they found at the crime scene matches a shoe they found in Roman's closet."

Quinn thought about her conversation with Roman the day

before, about how he'd said the cops hadn't found anything because there was nothing to find. Why had he lied to her? Or had he said what he did because he was innocent and knew the shoe wouldn't amount to anything? Or was Alicia mistaken?

"They shared custody of Jacob," Quinn said. "Roman was at Evie's house all the time. Makes sense there would a shoe print that matched one of his shoes."

"Think about it, Quinn," Astrid said. "First the shoe, now the life insurance policy. It's motive, if you ask me."

Quinn didn't believe it.

She couldn't.

"You don't know him," Quinn said. "Roman loved Evie."

"I'm just telling you what I heard, that's all."

"Dad, what does the call from Bo have to do with the life insurance policy?" Quinn asked.

"Roman ... he's ... well, there's no easy way to say this, Quinn."

"Dad, what's going on?"

"Bo called because he knew Jacob is here with you, and he, uhh, doesn't have your number."

"I still don't understand why he called you at all."

"He called to talk to me about Roman. He's dead, Quinn."

Roman's, ahh, he's dead. Bo stopped by his place this morning to ask him a few questions and—"

"Wait a minute. Why did Bo have questions for Roman?"

"I thought you knew. He's a detective now."

The news came as a surprise.

When they broke things off in high school, Quinn vowed to stay out of his life—and that included knowing anything about his life. She'd told her friends and family not to mention him to her. It was too hard, too painful. It brought up memories she still wasn't ready to face.

"As I was saying," her father continued, "when Bo arrived at

Roman's house, Roman's pickup was parked out front, but he didn't come to the door. They've always been good friends, so Bo announced himself and went inside. He found Evie's dog in the hallway outside Roman's room. Roman was on the bed, unresponsive. His body was stiff, cold to the touch. Bo checked for a pulse, and there wasn't one."

Quinn pressed a hand to her chest, struggling to breathe. "Do they know how he died?"

"Not for certain yet, but Bo did find a couple of pill bottles on the nightstand. Nembutal and fluoxetine hydrochloride."

"Fluoxe ... what?"

"One was for depression, the other to help him sleep."

"I don't understand. Are you saying Roman overdosed on pills?"

"Not just pills. There were beer cans all over the nightstand. Seems it's possible a combination of things led to his death. Guess we'll have to wait and see what the county coroner has to say."

"What does Bo think?"

"He believes Roman's death was an accident—not intentional as in suicide or murder—and I'm inclined to believe him."

11

Quinn knew what was coming next, knew *who* was coming, and it wasn't long before Bo pulled into her parents' driveway. Quinn took refuge in what her mother now called "the craft room," even though at one time, the room had been hers. She wanted a minute, just one minute to herself—to think, to breathe—but before she could get it, she felt a hand on her shoulder, and she jumped back.

"I need a minute, Astrid," Quinn said.

Astrid twirled a half-polished finger around a strand of hair. "Bo's here. He just pulled up."

"I'm aware."

"Have you talked to him … you know, since the two of you broke up?"

Not wanting to mention his short visit the night before, Quinn said, "I haven't."

"You should."

"I will when I'm ready," Quinn said.

"Dad, uhh, he said Marcus called yesterday to see how you're doing. He told me what happened between the two of you. You made the right decision by breaking things off. I never thought he was right for you."

Eugene entered the room and draped his arms around Astrid's shoulders. "What are you ladies talking about?"

"Nothing important," Quinn said. "If you'll excuse me, I need to check on Jacob."

Quinn exited the room, a rise of emotions mounting inside her like a wave ready to crest. It couldn't go up, only out, and she knew it. Eyes blurred with tears, she rushed down the hall, smacking right into Bo.

She wobbled back and mumbled an apology.

Bo reached out, trying to take her hand in his.

Unsure of whether to accept it, she kept her hands at her sides.

"Hey ... are you okay?" he asked.

Astrid looked around the corner, offering Bo a huge smile. "Well, hi there, stranger. Been a long time since we've seen each other."

"Uhh, yeah. Hey, Astrid."

His flat, emotionless words made it clear he wasn't happy to see her there.

"Quinn, your father told me he's talked to you about Roman," Bo said.

"I ... ahh, I can't do this right now," she said. "All of it, it's too much. I don't know how much more I can take. Evie's dead, and now Roman, and my life is ... and I just, I just, I can't ..."

A surge of emotions brewing from within was at its tipping point, and she couldn't, she wouldn't allow it to all come spilling out ... not in front of her sister, and not in front of *him*. She jerked to the side, sprinting down the hall as Bo chased after her.

"Quinn, stop," Bo said. "Please. Hold on a minute."

She made it outside the house and onto the front porch

before her legs buckled beneath her, a hand looping around her waist as she went down.

"I can't ... I can't breathe," she said.

"Yes, you can. Take it slow. I'll breathe with you, okay?"

She glanced up at him, and he said, "We're going to take a long breath in, hold it for a second, and then let it out. You ready?"

Quinn nodded, repeating the process several times before she felt her body begin to relax, the jittery nerves she'd been having slowing to a manageable rhythm.

"Thank you," she said. "I'm fine now. You can let go of me."

Their eyes locked, and he stared at her, saying nothing at first. Just when she thought it couldn't get any more awkward between them, he uttered something she didn't expect, "If I had it my way, I'd never let go of you again."

12

Quinn glanced through the windshield of her father's car, taking in the awe-inspiring view of the Shoshone River. Watching the gentle ease of the water's flow calmed her, uncluttering her mind. She loved this spot. It was *her* spot, the place she'd been coming to since she was old enough to drive. On this mountaintop, she could think, make decisions, make sense of things—when she was alone.

Except today she wasn't.

Quinn exited the vehicle and walked to the truck idling next to her, using her knuckles to tap on the driver's-side window.

The window lowered.

"Why did you follow me here?" Quinn asked.

"I wanted to make sure you were okay," Bo said. "I was hoping we could talk."

"Are you going to keep stopping by my parents' house until I do?"

"Will you ever talk to me if I don't?"

Good question.

Yesterday the answer would have been a firm *no*.

Now it was a pliable *maybe*.

"We're talking right now," she said.

"You know what I mean, Quinn."

"Why is it so important to you? We haven't spoken in years."

"If you wouldn't have avoided me for so long, we could have done this a long time ago."

"I thought about seeing you when I was in town from time to time. I just didn't know what I'd say if I did."

He reached behind him in the back seat, grabbing a blanket and holding it out to her. "Let's sit for a few minutes. I know how much you like it here. It's the perfect place for you to be right now. What do you say?"

She considered the suggestion, but she didn't take the blanket.

"I don't know. Jacob seemed all right to stay with my mom for a bit. He's down for a nap, but I should be there when he wakes up. I don't want him to worry."

"Jacob's in good hands. If he wakes up and needs you, your parents will call. You know they will." Bo got out of the truck, found a weedy patch of hillside, and spread the blanket out. "You coming?"

"How will talking now make things any different? We can't change the past."

"Change it, no—you're right. We can't. We can move on from it, though. It's long overdue, Quinn. I know it, and so do you."

She joined him, sitting on the far edge of the blanket.

He glanced at her, shaking his head as he laughed.

"What's so funny?" she asked.

"Nothing. Sit as far away from me as possible if you like. I'll take whatever I can get."

They sat in silence for a time, and then he scooted closer.

"Remember when we used to come here?" he asked.

Of course she remembered, and the memories were bittersweet, triggering a past she'd tried hard to forget. Sitting here now, she wondered if it had been wrong of her to work as hard as she had to wipe away the memories between them.

"When I think about the best moments of my life, aside from having my son, every single one of them was spent with you," she said.

He smiled at her, looking shocked by her admission.

"Can I ask you something?" he asked.

"I guess."

"Are you happy in your marriage?"

It was a subject she'd assumed would come up, but one she still wasn't prepared to talk about yet.

"I'm not," she said. "And I'd rather not talk about it."

"If you're not happy, why do you stay?" He paused, then added, "Sorry, you said you didn't want to talk about it. It's not right for me to push you. I meant no disrespect."

He was right.

He shouldn't have pushed the topic.

But something inside her felt it was just what she needed it.

"I left my husband," she said. "Once I get settled in and figure out where to go from here, I'll be hiring a lawyer and filing for divorce."

"I ... uhh, I heard about what happened to your son a while back. I'm sorry. You've been through so much then .. and now. Is there anything I can do?"

She wanted to say no, there was nothing he or anyone could do to make any of it go away. She'd been lying to herself all this time, running from her problems, resisting any opportunity to deal with them head on. Now, as she thought back on her life, she wondered if dealing with them was what she should have been doing all along.

"You want to talk about us, right?" she asked.

"I do."

"Fine, let's talk."

"Do you mean it? Are you sure?"

"Yeah, let's try at least."

Bo paused, then said, "I'm still not sure what happened to us, how it all fell apart. After you ended things, you took off on spring break. When you came back, it wasn't long before you were running around town with some other guy's ring on your finger. Every time I tried to talk to you about it, you shut me out. Then you married the guy and moved to Utah. After everything we had together, why did you do it? Why did you marry him?"

A window Quinn had long ago closed cracked open, and it was obvious Bo was working hard to keep it that way. Quinn assumed by now Bo would have married, had kids, but he hadn't. Nonetheless, she couldn't imagine being the reason he'd held back on those things.

Was she?

"You know why I ended our relationship," she said, choking on the words as she released them. "I saw you that night with my sister."

"I'll tell you now what I told you then—you have it all wrong," Bo said.

"I know what I saw."

"You didn't see what you think you did."

There was silence between them for a moment, and then she said, "I thought enough time has passed that I could have this conversation, but I'm not sure I can."

"Once, just once, talk to me, and I swear I'll never bring it up again."

Quinn crossed her arms, taking a deep breath in. "You kissed Astrid, and as if that wasn't enough, your hand was on her breast when I caught the two of you."

"You saw your sister kiss *me*, Quinn, not the other way around. Where was her hand when mine was over her chest? Do you even remember?"

As vivid as if it was happening in front of her now.

"Over yours," Quinn said. "What difference does it make?"

"Like I've always said, *she* kissed me. And I don't know why, but when she saw you coming, she took my hand and shoved it against her breast."

"Why would she do that?"

"I don't know. She blamed me for everything, and for whatever reason, you believed her. Even after I tried to explain myself, you took her side and then ran into the arms of some guy you didn't even know. You have no idea what that did to me."

"What was I supposed to do? You slept with her, Bo."

He threw his hands in the air, his head shaking. "I did *what*? Is that what she told you?"

"Yes."

"It's not true. What you saw that night was it. Nothing else happened, before or after. And it was never investigated by me, I assure you."

Looking at him now, seeing the sincerity in his eyes, she couldn't help but wonder if she'd made a mistake, a *big* mistake, one that had changed the course of her life.

Was there a chance she'd been that wrong?

"Astrid explained everything," Quinn said. "She might be a lot of things, but I can't believe she'd lie to me about the one thing she knew could hurt me most."

"I'm sorry to say it. She may be your sister, but this *is* Astrid we're talking about."

"It was more than words, though. Astrid had proof. It's why I believed her story over yours."

"What *proof?*"

"She showed me a note you wrote her that said you were breaking up with me to be with her."

Bo waved his hands in front of him. "Whoa. I don't know what you're talking about. I've never written Astrid a note in my life."

"I saw it with my own eyes. It was in your handwriting. There's no reason to deny it now."

"I'm telling you, it's not true," he said. "None of it. Not the note, not the groping, not the sex she says we had. I wouldn't ever do that to you, or any woman. I don't have it in me. You above everyone else should know I'm telling the truth. And you know something? I thought you knew me well enough to know the kind of person I am. Seems I thought wrong."

Was it possible her sister had been so cruel as to ruin their relationship without considering the aftermath? The damage? The shattered hearts and torn lives?

"I ... I don't know what to say," Quinn said.

"I don't know why your sister wanted to tear us apart," he said. "But whatever her reasons were, she succeeded."

"Messing with the lives of two people is a lot more than a silly joke. I can't believe she could be so vicious. I just can't."

"Ask yourself this—if I wanted to be with her, why didn't I get with her after you and I broke up? What was stopping us?"

"She said she saw you a few times, and then she started seeing someone else."

"Look at me, Quinn. If you ever loved me—"

His eyes glistened when they met hers, the same eyes she'd fallen in love with as a teen, eyes she'd never forgotten.

"When you found out I was marrying Marcus, why didn't you fight for me ... for us, for what we had?" Quinn asked.

"The way I saw it, if you loved me, you would have never married him in the first place."

It was a good point, one she hadn't considered before. Looking at Bo now, at his expression, so pained, so raw, one thing was clear: there was a good chance she'd been wrong ... wrong about everything.

13

Astrid and Eugene were parked in her parents' driveway, reclining back on the seats of his yellow convertible sportscar when Bo and Quinn returned to the house. Judging by the slurred sounds coming from Astrid's mouth when Quinn passed by, she'd downed more than her fair share of alcohol since they'd been gone, and it wasn't even dinnertime yet.

Astrid glanced up, her brow raised as if surprised to see Quinn and Bo together. "Well, well, well, look at that, the old love birds are talking again. How sweet."

Quinn turned toward Bo, head shaking. "Ignore her."

He leaned toward Quinn, lowering his voice to a whisper. "Astrid needs to come clean about what she did. She needs to admit she lied."

"I agree with you, but we should talk to her later, when she's sober."

Even when Astrid was sober, it never seemed like the right time to talk to her sister.

"Fine, we'll wait," he said. "Once she sobers up though, the three of us are having a chat."

"Bo, come here," Astrid said, waving him over. "I need to tell ya something."

"Maybe later."

"Oh, come on. I don't bite ... *most* of the time." She giggled. "Come here, talk to me. We haven't caught up in ages."

"It's best we catch up when you're not drinking."

"Do you think I'm drunk? I'm not drunk. *You're* drunk." Astrid slapped a hand to her leg, roaring with laughter. "Admit it, Bo. You're afraid to talk to me, aren't you?"

"Stop it, okay?" Bo said. "You're making a fool of yourself."

Eugene's mouth opened, and liquid courage came flowing out. "Hey, friend. Watch the way you're talking to my girl."

"I suggest you mind your own business, *friend*," Bo replied.

"Or what?"

"Are you mad at me, Bo?" Astrid pouted. "Because you seem a little mad. Why are you mad? Tell me, tell me, tell me."

Quinn and Bo exchanged glances, and Quinn recognized the look in his eye. The notion of waiting to talk to Astrid until she sobered up had been abandoned.

"You lied, Astrid," he said. "You ruined everything Quinn and I had built together. And for what? What did we ever do to you?"

Astrid shrugged. "I dunno what you're talking about. I did nothing, and I'm not saying nothing."

"Quinn needs to hear the truth."

"I'm not going to ask you again to watch your tone," Eugene said.

Bo stabbed a finger in Eugene's direction. "I suggest you stay out of it. This doesn't concern you."

"Well, that does it."

Eugene staggered as he attempted to get out of the car, the car door slamming behind him as he walked in Bo's direction.

"Wait ... hang ... hold on," Astrid said. "Everyone stop. I'll tell you what you want to know. Just stop, all of you."

Everyone froze, their eyes on Astrid, waiting to see what she was about to say next.

"It's true, Quinn," Astrid said. "I never slept with Bo. He never wanted to be with me."

"What's happening here?" Eugene asked. "What's this all about?"

Astrid slapped herself on the forehead. "Damn alcohol truth serum. Man, I'm going to regret this tomorrow."

"I don't understand, Astrid," Quinn said. "What about the note you showed me, the one that said he wanted to break up with me to be with you? It was in Bo's handwriting."

"I forged it. Traced over a letter he'd written you until I got his handwriting right."

"When did this happen?" Eugene asked.

"Years ago," Quinn said, "when we were all in high school."

Eugene crossed his arms, glared at Astrid. "Tell me you didn't. Tell me you wouldn't do something so cruel to your own sister."

Astrid turned toward Eugene and snorted a laugh. "Cruel? You want cruel? I thought I could love you, Eugene, with your receding hairline and dad bod. But you know what I love even more? Money. Money can make a 5 a 10, if I squint hard enough."

Stunned, Eugene stood there, jaw hanging open as if not knowing what to say.

"You ruined my life with your lie," Quinn said.

Astrid cocked her head to the side and burst into tears. "It was a stupid joke, Quinn. I never meant for it to go this long before I told you the truth. I'm sorry. I'm so, so sorry."

A joke?

Astrid's *joke* had upended Quinn's entire world, leading to a chain of events that altered the direction of her life.

"If you meant to tell me the truth, why didn't you?" Quinn asked.

"You *know* why."

Part of Quinn wanted to lash out, to wound her sister the way she'd been wounded.

But now wasn't the time.

Grabbing Bo's hand, she looked at him and said, "Let's go inside. We can sort the rest of this mess out later."

14

Quinn was sitting alone inside the casita, gazing at the shadowy figure looming in the hallway. It had been several hours since the fiasco in the driveway with Astrid, and it looked like it wasn't over yet.

"Don't you know how to knock?" Quinn asked.

A far more sober Astrid stepped into the light. "I ... I thought about it. You wouldn't have let me in if I did. I ... uhh, I know the door code, so I let myself in."

"Where's Eugene?"

"We had a fight, and he left. I figure he's back at the hotel, brooding. Who knows?" Astrid glanced around the room. "Where's Jacob?"

"Ruby asked if she could take him for the night. He was happy to see her, and he wanted to go, so I let him."

"Are you sure that's a good idea?"

Determined to honor both Evie and Roman's memory, Quinn had spoken to Ruby about pressing Jacob for information he wasn't ready to give. Ruby promised it wouldn't happen again, and Quinn wanted to believe her. Even if she didn't, she had no legal right keeping him from her. While Ruby proved to be a wild card at times, she was still Jacob's great-grandmother.

"Why are you here, Astrid?" Quinn asked.

"Now that I confessed what I did, do you hate me?"

Quinn looked over at her sister. Her expression had softened, not to the point of full remorse, but it was teetering. She thought about the first time she taught her to ride a bike, and the time Astrid discovered a snake slithering through the grass in the backyard. Astrid had been so scared. And even though their mother had been close by, it was Quinn's arms she'd run to for safety.

Where had it all gone wrong?

"I have every right to hate you, but I don't," Quinn said. "Whatever grievances we've had in the past, no matter how angry I am or have been, you're still my sister. I am angry, though. What you did … it wasn't right. I'd never do something like that to another person, let alone my own sister."

"I know, and you're right. The lie snowballed so fast, and it got out of hand. I've wanted to tell you the truth for years. I meant it when I said I'm sorry, Quinn."

Quinn let out a long, frustrated breath. "It's been a long day, and I'm tired."

Astrid leaned against the wall, crossing her arms in front of her. "I came over because I was hoping you'd let me explain myself, explain why I did what I did."

"You should have come to me with an explanation a long time ago."

"I know. I'm coming to you now, at least."

"I'm not sure I'm up for a serious conversation tonight."

Astrid nodded. "Okay, yeah. I get it."

"How long are you going to be here?"

"I don't know. Mom and Dad want me to stick around for a bit. Well, that was before. Mom overheard the conversation we had outside earlier, and she's disappointed in me, to say the least. Dad sat me down, and we talked. He wants me to make things right. Well, his exact words were—'*you have to make it right*,' and I will. But if you want to wait, let's wait. We'll talk more when you're ready."

Astrid half-turned like she was waiting for Quinn to stop her, to offer up the kind of compassion she'd always given her sister in the past, but Quinn wasn't in a compassionate mood.

"I guess I'll go now," Astrid said. "Goodnight."

"Hold on."

Astrid turned, eyes wide, full of hope.

"Bo was everything I had ever wanted in a man, Astrid," Quinn said. "He was my whole life, the only man who has ever loved me for me. Whatever your reasons were for doing what you did, I do know one thing—I didn't deserve it. Even if I hear you out, you'll have to earn your way back into the inner circle of my life. Right now, you're about the farthest thing from it."

15

"I thought I knew you, but based on your behavior tonight, it's obvious I don't," Eugene said.

"I was drunk," Astrid replied. "I didn't mean what I said about you. I like you, Eugene. I have since the moment we met."

Eugene shoved some clothes into a suitcase and turned, glaring at Astrid. "I don't believe you, and the thing is, you wouldn't be the first person to like me for my money. Doesn't matter anymore. This is over ... *we're* over."

Watching him stumble around the room, it was obvious he'd kept the liquor flowing well into the night.

"Eugene, I—"

He raised a hand. "Save it. You've been using me this entire time, spending my money like water in a sieve, and I'm a fool because I let you. I thought you were different, but you're not. You're just like all the rest."

"Oh, come on. You know I say stupid things sometimes when I'm drinking."

Eugene whipped around, slapping Astrid across the face.

The force of it knocked her off balance, and she dropped to the floor.

He leaned over her, growling, "Oh, you meant every single word. You just didn't expect it to spill out of your mouth when it did."

Stunned, Astrid remained silent, her hand pressed to her cheek as she thought back to their first dinner date together. She'd been cornered in the ladies' room by a much older woman. The woman had noticed Astrid dining with Eugene and had felt the need to warn her. According to the woman, Eugene had dated her friend, Carla. After a nasty argument one night, he'd slapped Carla around. The following day Carla reported the incident to the police, but Eugene had gotten to them already. They were convinced Carla had abused *him*, and that he was only defending himself. Eugene had a black eye to prove it, one Carla told friends he'd given himself.

After hearing the woman's story, Astrid mentioned the conversation to Eugene. He laughed it off, saying the woman was a liar. He swore he'd never laid a hand on a woman in his life, and Astrid believed him. Now, on the floor and in a tremendous amount of pain, she wished she'd heeded the woman's words of warning.

"You thought you could play with my emotions," Eugene hissed. "What was your plan? Stay with me until you bled me dry and then skip out one day when I wasn't around?"

Astrid had never seen this side of him before—the furrowed brow, the tight lips, the sinister man hiding beneath the playful exterior. How could she have? She hadn't known him long enough to notice anything other than what she always did in a man—the same addictive seduction that gripped her time and time again.

Prestige.

Power.

Money.

A toxic combination she couldn't resist.

"I'm hurt, Eugene," she said.

"I'm *hurt*, Eugene," he mocked. "You'll live."

"I no longer feel safe around you. I want to leave."

"You'll leave when I say you can."

Astrid tried to stand, and he hit her again, harder this time.

"Stop it, Eugene! Touch me again, and I'll ... I'll call the police!"

"Call the police if you like. They won't believe a word you say."

"Bo will believe me."

Eugene laughed. "After the lies you told, I doubt he'd have any interest in helping you. Even if he did, my lawyer would shut him down. By the time he'd be done with you, everyone would see you for who you are—a drunk, incompetent harlot."

Astrid's legs wobbled as she tried to stand, pressing a hand against the top of her knee to boost herself up.

She started for the door, and he rushed after her, fists clenched, ready to strike.

He was going to hit her a third time.

She was sure of it.

Her eyes glassed the room, coming to rest on a crystal candy dish.

So hard, so heavy, so round.

So ... perfect.

If she could knock him off his feet, she could get away.

Astrid curled her fingers around the textured glass and swung. The bowl smashed into the side of his head, and he staggered back. Stumbling over his pant leg, he hit the ground, and the sound of his head cracking against the floor echoed throughout the room.

She'd hit him a lot harder than intended.

And he wasn't moving.

She leaned forward, "Eugene?"

He remained quiet and still.

Astrid considered prodding him with a finger to see if he'd move but she resisted. She'd seen enough movies to predict the usual outcome of situations like this one. The moment she got close enough, he'd spark back to life, take hold of her ankle, and down she'd go. Before he regained consciousness, she needed to grab her stuff and get out of there.

She raced toward the bedroom, her eyes darting around the space until they found her handbag. She slung it over her shoulder and walked toward the hotel room door, glancing back on her way out. What she saw was unexpected. Blood had seeped onto the floor from a cut in Eugene's head. She didn't know whether the glass dish or the floor was to blame ... or whether it was a bit of both. Either way, she knew she was in trouble.

Big trouble.

In a panic, she pulled out her cell phone, pressing on a picture of a familiar face. The phone rang four times and then went to voicemail. She ended the call and dialed again. She'd dial a thousand times if necessary—she just had to get through.

Please, please, pick up the phone.

Three tries later, the call was answered with a stiff, emotionless, "Why are you calling me at this—?"

"Quinn ..."

"It's two in the morning, Astrid. What is it?"

"It's Eugene. I think he's ... I mean ... he seems, umm ..."

"He seems like what?"

"I ... I think he's dead."

16

D*ead.*

The word jolted Quinn from a sound sleep, and she propped herself into a sitting position. "Tell me what happened."

"I went to the hotel to get my stuff," Astrid said. "I thought Eugene would either be asleep or he would have packed his stuff and left, but he was there, and he wasn't happy to see me."

"And?"

"We got into an argument, and he said it was over. He accused me of being with him for his money, and then he slapped me a couple of times."

"He *hit* you?"

"Yep."

"Then what?"

"I tried to leave. He said I couldn't until he let me. I ran toward the door, and he chased after me. I figured he was going to hit me again, so I grabbed a glass dish and smashed it over his head. He fell, and it looks like he cracked his head open. He hasn't moved since. Oh, and there's blood, lots of it, kinda pooling around his head and stuff."

"How long ago did this happen?"

"Five minutes or so."

"Have you touched him, checked to see if he has a pulse?" Quinn asked. "Are you sure he's dead?"

"Are you kidding me? I'm not going anywhere near the guy."

"You called 9-1-1, right?"

Silence.

"Astrid, please tell me you made the call," Quinn said.

"I ... well, I was going to, but then I started thinking ... What if they don't understand it was an accident?"

"It doesn't matter. Hang up and dial 9-1-1. You don't have a choice. Say there's been an accident, and you need an ambulance right away."

"What if they don't believe my story?"

"Make the call, Astrid. You'll look suspicious if you don't. They can look at your phone records and see you called me first instead of reporting it. So, do it. You don't need to worry about your story, because when they get there, you're not going to say anything."

"How's that going to work?"

"Trust me and do what I'm asking you to do. When the police and the paramedics arrive, let them in and escort them to Eugene. Beyond that, if they press with you with personal questions, don't say anything incriminating. Tell them what you told me, nothing more, and be sure to say you only did what you did to defend yourself. If they press you further or ask to take you down to the police department for questioning, tell them you're waiting to speak with your lawyer."

"Okay, but I don't have a lawyer."

"You will," Quinn said. "I'll talk to Dad. He'll know what to do."

"I'm scared. I've never ... killed a person before."

"You don't know he's dead. For all you know, you just knocked the guy out."

"What if he *is* dead, though? I can't stop trembling. I'm scared. I'm so scared."

"I know, but right now, you need to pull yourself together. It's going to be okay."

"Will you come to the hotel? Please? Just this once. I can't do this alone, and I know I don't deserve your time, but if you come, I'll never ask you for another favor again. I swear it."

A Bible verse popped into Quinn's mind from the book of Matthew. Something about turning the other cheek. It seemed like God expected a lot more than she was capable of at times. When it came to her past with Astrid, Quinn didn't just feel she'd been slapped on the cheek, she felt they'd been beaten. Her face burned with anger just thinking about it.

But Astrid was her sister.

And no matter what had happened between them, just for tonight, her own grievances from the past needed to be put to the side.

17

Much to Astrid's surprise, and relief, Eugene *wasn't* dead. The blood seeping from his head was more of a pooling of drips than the leaky faucet Astrid described. And for once, Astrid heeded Quinn's advice, not saying much to the police about what happened until the lawyer arrived, a woman named Carolyn Adair, who'd been hired by her father.

Carolyn arrived at the hotel in a Jaguar. The frame around her license plate read: *My other ride is a broom.* Quinn didn't doubt it. One look at the woman's shrewd, cat-framed glasses and pressed pantsuit, and she had every reason to believe Astrid was going to be fine.

It was seven o'clock in the morning when Quinn returned home. She considered sleep, even if all she managed was a few minutes of it. But she didn't sleep. Her mind was wired, too caught up in recent events to allow for even the smallest escape.

Making her way to the kitchen, Quinn stretched her arms above her head and yawned. Stuck to the refrigerator was a note, and her name was written on the front in thick, hot-pink marker. She recognized the handwriting as Astrid's, and she assumed Astrid must have found a way to leave it the night before, prior to going to the hotel.

She brewed a cup of coffee and sat at the table, staring at the letter for a time before opening it. Then her impatience got the better of her, and she unfolded it and began to read.

Quinn,

I've always planned on telling you the truth about Bo. I meant to tell you right after it happened, and then I thought about how angry you would be if I did. The longer I waited, the harder it was for me to come right out and admit what I did, and why. Our relationship back then ... well, it was already strained. I thought once I came clean, you'd never talk to me again. Now I realize, we don't talk all that much anyway, and I know it's my fault.

When I look back now, I know my actions were childish, stupid, and wrong. I know I hurt you, and I know I hurt Bo, all because of my own selfishness. You don't have to forgive me. Truth is, I've never forgiven myself. But I'll promise you this—I'll never lie to you again.

And while this letter is meant as an apology, I'm not the only one who's been keeping a secret all these years. You've kept a secret from someone too. If I'm willing to admit the truth, maybe one day you can do the same. You should talk to Bo. He deserves to know what happened after the breakup. Maybe if you let him in, there's still a chance the two of you can get back on track. I hope so.

Astrid

P.S. Marcus is a loser. He wasn't good to you, not in the way you deserve. I've always wanted to tell you that too.

P.S.S. I really am sorry.

Quinn flattened the note on the table in front of her, poring over Astrid's words once more before shoving the letter to the side.

So much had changed in such a short time, the guilt of past mistakes springing forth again, reminding her of what life could have been like if only things had been different. If she had listened to Bo when he'd proclaimed his innocence, where would they be now?

No matter.

It was all in the past, and though the last week had been an unhealthy blend of dramatic ends and heartfelt beginnings, today was different.

Today was a chance to begin anew.

While lacking in sleep, Quinn felt invigorated and gutsy, like a woman on a mission. It had taken years for her to stand up to Marcus, to end a union that never should have started in the first place.

Marcus and Astrid weren't the only two people who had pushed Quinn around. A murderer had taken from her the one person she valued most. Evie had always been there for Quinn, always protecting her. Now it was Quinn's turn to do the same.

18

Evie's quaint, two-bedroom house was located at the end of an unpaved road that backed against a steep, tree-filled mountainside. The square, red-brick house with white wooden shutters wasn't new, and it wasn't big, but it was what Evie had always referred to as her own private slice of heaven. While outspoken in temperament, Evie had always preferred simple country living to a fast-paced life on a street chockful of cookie-cutter homes.

Given Evie's need for solitude, it didn't surprise Quinn when she bought the place on Duggar Road from a retired couple who'd called it home for over forty-five years. Evie's closest neighbor, Norma Healy, lived several acres away. Norma's elaborate, two-story house with floor-to-ceiling windows was visible from Evie's front yard, but still far enough of a distance to give Evie the privacy she desired. Given this fact, and the fact Norma was in her upper eighties and wore hearing aids, it made sense when Norma told police she hadn't heard any gunshots ring out on the night Evie was murdered.

Quinn exited the car, taking in the surroundings. Evie's place fit the bill of an active murder scene to a tee. Yellow crime-scene tape was still affixed to the front door, and the flower garden was disheveled, flowers withering from too many days of inconsistent watering. Evie had always been meticulous about her flowerbeds, and at this moment, it looked as though a herd of animals had barreled right through them. Quinn assumed the "herd" was the cops, combing through the yard in the hopes of finding clues to Evie's murder.

Had any been found, she wondered?

In the far corner of the yard, Evie's Harley-Davidson Heritage Softail rested beneath a carport next to a restored Mustang. The bike was the first thing Evie bought when the business started to take off. Now, it looked abandoned and forsaken, much like the rest of the place.

Quinn entered the house, noticing Evie's computer had been removed from the desk. Only shapes remained on its surface, areas where Evie hadn't dusted. Quinn pressed her hands into the soft, fine-grain leather of Evie's couch and thought back to the last time she'd sat there.

Several months before, Quinn had flown in to surprise Evie on her birthday. The house was filled with laughter then, and Evie seemed happier than usual. She told Quinn she was dating someone new. A man named Ray Ferguson, a transplant from Texas. He had just moved to Cody to accept a job as a hatchery manager, a person in charge of incubating trout eggs and then transferring them to local lakes and streams in the area. From what Evie said about him, he sounded like a standup guy with a standup job.

But was he?

Quinn's focus shifted to a kid's puzzle laid out on the coffee table. The scene on the box lid depicted a playful group of safari animals. The puzzle had almost been finished, save a few pieces. Quinn stared at it, wondering where Jacob had been when Evie was murdered.

Had he been in the room she was in now, working on the puzzle?

A few feet away, large stains on a rug inside the bathroom caught her eye. Quinn started for the room and then stopped, concerned she wouldn't be able to bring herself to look inside.

When she'd made the decision to visit Evie's house earlier that morning, she thought she was prepared. Now she knew she wasn't. Even so, she took a deep breath in and kept going.

Entering the bathroom, she dropped to her knees over the rug. The stains were now a dark, purplish black, the result of the blood blending with the colors in the rug. She pressed both hands into the center of the stain, sobbing as she thought about what Evie must have endured in the final moments of her life. As the tears rolled down Quinn's cheeks, a female voice jolted her from her thoughts.

"I don't think you're supposed to be here."

A cold shiver surged through Quinn's body as she stood and turned. The woman behind her stepped forward, gave her a small smile, and then stared down at the rug.

"I don't think you're supposed here either, Mrs. Healy," Quinn said.

Mrs. Healy narrowed her eyes, nodding. "At my age, I don't much care about what's right or wrong anymore. Truth is, this isn't the first time I've been here since Evie died. I've driven over a few times. I tried to water the garden, but the darn spigot was screwed on too tight. Couldn't get it to budge."

"It was nice of you to try."

"I know how much Evie's flower garden meant to her. Be a real shame to let it all die out."

Quinn crossed her arms. "I didn't see you at the funeral."

"I planned to attend, but that morning, I woke up feeling like I had a chest cold. Decided it would be best to stay in bed. Besides, she wouldn't have known I was there. Sad as it is, she's gone now. Best to accept it and move on. Some people believe the spirit of a person lingers, even after death. Not me. Ashes to ashes, as they say."

"Oh, I don't know," Quinn replied. "My parents brought me up to believe there was another life after this one."

"I don't mean to dissuade you from what you've been taught, dear, but I see it in a different way. I believe the moment death takes us, life starts again, gives us a new beginning, a second or a third chance to be someone else, do things we missed this time around."

"Reincarnation?"

"If that's what you want to call it."

Reincarnation.

Quinn didn't believe in it.

She wasn't fond of the idea of evolution either.

"Mrs. Healy, were you at home the night Evie died?" Quinn asked.

"I'm home every evening. At my age, I see no point going out anymore."

"I know your house is a short distance from here, but is there any chance you remember seeing ... something, anything? No matter how unimportant it may seem."

"Police asked me the same question. Asked me a lot of other things, too."

"So *did you* see anything?"

"You're well aware Evie's visitors had to cross in front of my house in order to get back here, and though it's hard for me to get my days straight sometimes, I did recall seeing two pickup trucks pass in front of my house that night."

"What time?"

"I don't know. Once it gets dark, I don't pay much mind."

"If it was dark outside, how do you know it was two trucks and not the same one coming and going?"

For that matter, Quinn wondered how Mrs. Healy could have differentiated a truck from a car or a van, even.

"The trucks were different from each other," Mrs. Healy said.

"In what way?"

Mrs. Healy sighed, closing her eyes like she regretted being there. "The first truck was Roman's. He stopped by often to see Jacob. I always knew when it was him because his headlights were round, and when it was dark, he always had his darned brights turned on."

"And the second vehicle?"

"The other truck belonged to the new fellow she'd been seeing. Think she said his name was Jay."

Close.

"Ray," Quinn corrected.

"That's right. The headlight on his passenger side is busted. I kept needling Evie to get after him to get it fixed. He never did, though."

"Was Ray the first or second visitor that night?"

"I can't say for certain."

"Were you watching television at the time?" Quinn asked. "Maybe if you recall what show was on, it would help establish a timeline."

"I watched a lot of things that night."

Quinn was getting nowhere.

She switched gears.

"There's a rumor going around that Roman was a suspect," Quinn said.

Mrs. Healy shrugged. "No surprise there. He didn't like the fact that Evie was seeing someone new. Ask me, Roman had a bit of a jealous streak."

"What about the new guy—what do you think of him?"

"Seemed nice enough. He was a quiet fellow. Never said more than a few words to me when I saw him."

"Have you told all this to the police?"

"I told them a few things. Not much. I don't like the way they came around here, poking and prodding me for answers, asking me the same questions over and over, like I'll come up with something new to say on their fourth or fifth try. I'm old, not stupid."

"I'm sure they're just doing their best to find out what happened."

"I get the feeling they think I'm lying, like I saw something, and I refuse to say."

The police had good reason to be suspicious of Mrs. Healy. Several years earlier, a rumor had gone around town that Mrs. Healy's husband had died under mysterious circumstances after he fell from a tractor—one he'd operated so many times, Quinn was sure he could have done it blindfolded. Her husband's brother suspected foul play on her part, but the allegations were never proven.

Standing before her now, Quinn couldn't imagine the wrinkly-faced, curly-haired woman was capable of such a thing —murder—except for one small infraction. There was something about the way her eyes scampered around when she talked, never settling on any one thing. It seemed suspicious, but was it? Or was Quinn creating her own narrative, one that didn't exist?

19

"Can I come in?" Quinn asked.

Bo held the screen door open with one hand and gripped a can of Mountain Dew in the other. "Sure, it's nice to see you."

Quinn ducked under his outstretched arm and entered the living room, checking out the sparse surroundings. In terms of furniture, Bo was a minimalist. There was a set of distressed-leather couches in a rusty brown color and a single end table with a simple, black lamp on top. No flat-screen TV. No state-of-the-art stereo. Not in the living room, at least. What he did have was books. His shelves were brimming with them. Hemingway, Doyle, Fleming. Most of the greats were there, all lined side by side in alphabetical order according to the last name of the author.

"You don't own a television?" Quinn asked.

"You seem surprised."

"Guess I shouldn't be. I don't remember us watching TV together when we dated."

"We didn't. We found far more productive ways to spend our time."

He grinned, his eyes glazing over like he'd been sucked into a distant memory. She was curious as to which one might have sprung to mind.

"You're working Evie's murder investigation, right?" Quinn asked.

"I am."

"Cool."

Cool?

It seemed like such a strange thing to say but given so many years had passed since they'd spoken, her nerves were getting the better of her.

Quinn reached into the pocket of her oversized cardigan, pulling out a pint jar, which she set down on the end table. "My mom asked me to give you this strawberry jam. She remembers how much you liked it when we were younger."

"How sweet. Thank her for me, would you?"

"I will."

They stared at each other for a time, and she stuck out a hand. As soon as the gesture was made, she cringed, feeling like an idiot. But was too late to take it back now. She'd committed, and there it was, dangling in front of him.

Bo stared at the outstretched hand, his expression a combination of uneasiness and confusion. "Ehh, what are you doing?"

"We're shaking."

"On what?"

"Our friendship."

He smiled. "Our friendship? That's what we are now? Friends?"

"I'd like to be friends. I mean, if you want to be."

The longer her hand went unaccepted, the weirder the moment became. She pulled back, and he reached out, flattening it between both of his own.

"What are you doing, Quinn?"

"What do you mean?"

"You come over here, give me a jar of strawberry jam, offer to be friends again. You want something … and don't bother denying it. I can tell."

She sighed, realizing he was still great at reading her. "All right, fine. The truth is, I would like us to be friends."

"*And*? What else do you want?"

"Would you be willing to tell me what you know so far about Evie's murder?"

He released her hand. "I can't talk to you about it."

"Oh, come on, Bo. You can. You just won't."

"I understand how frustrating everything is right now. I need you and everyone else in this town to be patient. Trust in the system. We know what we're doing. I know you, and I know how you think. You want to be involved in the case, but I don't want you any more involved than you have to be. I'm not trying to be a jerk. I'm trying to look out for you."

"You know how much Evie meant to me. I hoped I would be able to leave it alone, to just let the investigation play out, but it's too hard for me to sit around and not do anything. I'm sorry, I just can't."

He crossed his arms, tipping his head toward her. "When you say you *can't*, what does that mean? What have you been doing?"

"I may have stopped by Evie's house before I came here."

Bo shook his head. "You shouldn't have gone over there."

"I know, but I did. At least I'm admitting it."

"You saw the crime-scene tape on the door, right?"

Quinn nodded.

"Did you touch anything while you were there?" he asked.

"No. Well, not much."

"Which is it—yes or no?"

"I had to move the tape so I could get inside the house. I stuck it back up when I left."

"I guess it didn't occur to you that we left the tape up for a reason."

"It's to keep people from going in her house, right?"

"Wrong. We left it up so we'd know if anyone has been to the house since we left. Sometimes killers return to the scene of the crime."

"Why?" she asked.

"For one, it allows them to relive the experience. For two, their own paranoia often convinces them they left something behind that they shouldn't have. Things like hair or fingerprints. Sometimes they go back to double check."

It was something Quinn had never considered. "I'm sorry, Bo. None of those things occurred to me."

"How did you get in?"

Quinn dug into her front pocket, fished out a silver piece of metal, and held it in front of him.

"You have a key to Evie's house?" he asked.

It was more of a statement than a question.

"I've always had one," she said. "Ever since Evie bought the place."

"I see."

He went quiet for so long the silence had become uncomfortable.

What was he thinking?

Was he mad, frustrated with her because she'd entered the house?

"Look, I'd like to stay and talk, but I have an appointment soon," she said.

"You just got here."

"I never planned on staying long. I know you're busy investigating Evie's murder."

"Are you leaving because I won't talk to you about the case?"

"It's like I just said: I have an appointment."

Bo raised a suspicious brow. "With whom?"

She started for the door and said, "Why does it matter?"

"Is it a secret meeting?"

"If you must know, I have an appointment with your father. He needs to go over Evie's will with me."

Bo nodded. "Ahh, right."

Quinn turned, walking toward the door. When she got there, she turned back. "I'm looking for answers about Evie's murder, just like you. Please don't ask me to leave it alone, Bo. I need to know she didn't die for nothing."

"I understand how you feel, and I know you came here for answers. I can't give you any yet. I hope you understand."

"I do. I just hoped maybe you'd give me a little bit of information to, uh, keep me in the loop, I guess. I get it, but I don't like it."

"Promise me you'll leave it to me, okay? We don't know who murdered Evie or why. The last thing I want is for Evie's killer to get wind that you've been snooping around."

A part of her wanted to say yes, to give him a verbal agreement that she'd stay out of it, allowing Bo and the police force to do their job. The other part was restless with a single, unwavering objective, one that wasn't going away—the need to find Evie's killer, sooner than later.

20

Bo's father rose from his chair and smiled. "Nice to see you, Quinn. Glad you got my message."

"Good to see you too," Quinn said. "It's been a long time, Mr. McCallister."

He swished a hand through the air. "Call me Edward."

Edward was dressed in a simple charcoal suit, nothing flashy or fancy, and scuffed loafers. It wasn't because he couldn't afford better ones. He could afford just about anything he wanted. Aside from his law practice, he'd inherited a vast amount of land from his father, which he'd subdivided and sold over the years. He just chose not to spend much of the money he made. He stashed it away, choosing to invest, make money with money. And even though he was financially secure, he still maintained his business, which Quinn found impressive.

"I'm glad to see you haven't retired yet," Quinn said.

"Oh, I've scaled back a fair amount over the past couple of years. I work about four months a year now, unless I have a client with pressing needs. I've given some thought to the idea of shutting the business down, but work suits me. Always has, I suppose. I'm married to it. In a lot of ways, a job is like a wife, like that old Led Zeppelin song, 'I Can't Quit You Baby.'"

They both laughed.

Aside from Bo, Edward and his wife had three other children, all boys. Bo was the baby of the family and had come along almost a decade after his brothers, a welcome, though unexpected surprise.

Edward gestured to a pair of brown leather chairs in front of his desk and said, "Take a seat, and we can talk about Evie's will."

"I'd like to discuss something with you after, something unrelated to Evie, if it's okay," she said.

"Sure, sure. Let's get right to it, then, shall we? The first thing I should mention is that Evie left her landscaping business to you."

Quinn pressed a hand to her check, gasping.

She knew almost nothing about landscaping or lawn maintenance ... or running a business, for that matter.

"I take it she never mentioned her wishes about the business to you," he said.

"Not a word. To say I'm inexperienced in her line of work would be a gross understatement."

"I'm sure her staff can assist you, show you the ropes. Then you'll need to decide what you want to do."

"What I want to do? What are my options?"

"You're either going to keep the business or sell it," he said.

Evie had cultivated and grown the business from nothing. It didn't seem right for Quinn to sell it. She assumed when Evie made the decision to leave it to her, she'd done it as a precaution, thinking she'd live long enough to own it until she retired.

And then fate stepped in.

"Can I ask you a question?" Quinn asked.

"Anything."

"Why do you think she left the business to me?"

Edward grabbed a folder off his desk, opened it, and pulled out an envelope. He handed it to her and said, "She told me to give you this if anything happened to her. When she wrote it, she never thought the day would come when I'd be sitting here, handing it to you. It was written just in case, and now ... well, I'm glad she took the time to write it."

Quinn stared at the envelope, at her name written in large, cursive letters.

"Have you read it?" she asked. "Do you know what it says?"

"It was sealed when she brought it to me. We did not discuss its contents. I tucked it away in her file, hoping I'd never have to hand it off to you. She left one for Roman too. Shame."

"When were the letters written?"

"Right after her divorce from Roman was finalized. Evie said she'd decided never to marry again, and she wanted to make sure things were taken care of in the event of her ... well, you know."

Quinn closed her eyes, feeling anxious and sick to her stomach. None of this seemed real, and yet it *was* real. She wasn't just stepping into Evie's life. She was assuming it. She folded the envelope in half and slipped it inside her purse.

"I suppose we should talk about Jacob," she said.

"Are you aware of Evie's wishes for the boy?"

"I am. Evie gave me a copy of the letter of consent when she wrote it. The letter stated if anything ever happened to both her and Roman, I was to become Jacob's guardian."

"Is this something you want and are prepared to accept?"

Quinn leaned back, crossing one leg over the other. "I'd do anything for Evie, and for Jacob. It's one of those things you agree to, thinking it's nothing but a formality."

"And now that it's more than that?"

. . .

"I want to do right by him, of course. I just hope I can help him through this, raise him in a way that would make Evie and Roman proud."

"I have no doubt you will."

"All that's happened in the past several days feels like a dream ... a horrible, awful dream."

"The death of a loved one is a long process sometimes, Quinn. There's no rush, no right way to do things, and there's no time limit on grieving. It requires patience. You'll get through this in your own way, and in your own time."

What about Jacob?

Would *he*?

"What needs to happen before I'm granted custody?" she asked.

Edward opened the top drawer of his desk, slid the folder inside, and closed it. "The process isn't hard, and it shouldn't take long. We'll need to file a petition with the court stating your interest in becoming Jacob's legal guardian. We'll also present the letter of consent. The judge will take it all into consideration and rule in the best interest of the child. Then he will approve the guardianship petition. I'll stay in touch, so you know how it's going. In the meantime, you said you had something to discuss with me. What is it I can do for you?"

"I need some legal advice, and I wasn't sure who to ask."

"Go on."

"I left my husband, Marcus, last week."

He raised a brow, which told Quinn he wasn't aware they'd split. "Are you wanting a trial separation, or a legal separation, or are you wanting to get a divorce?"

"It's over between us," she said. "I don't want to leave things open-ended, not even for a short time. I'd like to file for divorce."

Edward leaned forward in his chair, tapping a finger on the edge of the desk. "Are you sure?"

His concern was genuine, but his face also expressed something more—*hope*.

Quinn had spent a fair amount of time at Bo's house in high school, and Edward had given her advice on a couple of occasions. She'd always felt a closeness with Bo's parents, and there was a time when Edward had expressed how much he hoped Bo and Quinn would have a future together.

After all these years, was it possible he still felt the same way?

"You've had a tough week," Edward said. "You sure you don't need a moment to let it all settle in first?"

Quinn went quiet for a moment and then said, "I've wanted the relationship to be over for a while. I just didn't have the courage to end things, not until now. All I want is to be free of my husband. I'm just not sure how to go about it."

"It's easy to get the ball rolling. What concerns do you have?"

"Marcus is a lawyer. He works for a prestigious law firm in Utah. I'm worried he is going to do everything he can to stall the divorce or to find a way to keep all our assets. The truth is, I'd leave everything to him if it meant I'd be free."

"Have you told him the relationship is over?"

"I have," she said.

"How did he react?"

"He didn't accept it at first. He didn't think I was serious. I expect it's because I ended things right after I found out Evie died. He thought I wasn't thinking straight."

"And now?"

"I'm not sure where his head's at. We haven't spoken a word, not since I left."

Edward paused a moment, taking it all in. "Not to worry. I

have a friend, a fellow colleague I work with on occasion. He lives in Utah, so he'll be able to represent you there. Marcus may believe he has the upper hand right now, but this colleague of mine is one of the top divorce attorneys in the state. I'll get in touch with him and give him your information so he can contact you. Sound good?"

Quinn stood, feeling a rush relief sweep over her. "Sounds great. Thank you for your help. When it comes to my past and some of the decisions I've made, I'm embarrassed and ashamed. I've made so many mistakes. I wish I could go back and do it all over again."

"I have lived on this earth a lot longer than you, kiddo, and let me tell you something ... You'll continue to make mistakes, even when you get to my age. There's no need to beat yourself up over the past. Think of it this way—your past taught you a valuable lesson. Learn from it and move on. That's what matters most. Focus on the person you are today, the person sitting in front of me, right here, right now."

It was sound advice.

Quinn nodded, stood, and walked to the door, hesitating before she made her exit. There was a burning question she wanted to ask, if she dared ask it. It was the same nagging question that had plagued her since she'd entered Edward's office.

And now it was festering.

"If you don't mind me asking, why hasn't Bo ever married?"

Edward tapped a pencil to the top of his desk, thinking, like he was trying to form not just *any* answer, but the right one.

"You're here now," he said. "Why don't you ask him yourself?"

"I'm not sure I can. After what happened between us, I feel like I don't have the right."

"Why let your previous actions stop you from taking the opportunity you have to change things now?"

He was right.

She'd spent too much of her life keeping things in, not dealing with life's problems. It seemed easier that way. But was it?

"Thank you for saying what I needed to hear," she said.

Edward stood and walked over, reaching out and taking her hands in his. "We never understood what happened between the two of you back then. And yes, we were hopeful it would work itself out. The break-up was hard on Bo, I'll admit. He wouldn't talk about it, and we didn't push. We just let it be. We knew he'd find his way through it, and he did."

"If you don't mind me asking, how do you feel Bo's doing now?"

"He's been on a lot of first dates, not many second ones. No relationships, at least no one he's ever brought around for more than a quick hello. When my wife asks him about it, he always says the same thing—women are different now."

Different?

What did that mean?

"I want him to be happy," Quinn said. "I can't tell if he is or not."

"Since we're exchanging information, I wonder if you might indulge a curious father by answering a question of mine. You're back in town, and from what I gather, you've seen Bo a few times now. Is it possible you still have feelings for my son?"

Was it possible?

Good question.

She just wasn't sure she knew the answer.

21

Ruby plunged her rubber-gloved hands into the murky, debris-filled water in the kitchen sink and picked up the same white plate for a third time. At this point, it was so clean, it sparkled like her floors did after a good polish. If she looked at the plate close enough, she could even make out the shadowy outline of her own reflection.

The ritual of standing at the counter, circling her hand around a thrice-cleaned plate had little to do with cleanliness and a lot more to do with resisting the urge to do something else—something she'd promised to *stop* doing—pressing Jacob for information. The fact he wasn't speaking weighed on her mind. She wished she knew what he was thinking or how he was feeling.

If she pushed him again, it was possible she'd do more damage than good.

Still, the urge was there.

Ruby's thoughts turned to Evie.

It wasn't right that she was dead, and Ruby was still alive.

It went against the natural order of things.

Popping her head into the living room, Jacob looked up

at her from his spot at the coffee table where he'd spent most of the morning drawing. She offered him a warm smile. Part of her felt guilty standing there, contemplating ideas on how to get him talking, and a thought came to mind. Maybe the reason he wasn't talking was because he was *suppressing* something—something he needed to get out.

Could it be true?

Was it possible that opening him up could help him in some way?

Jacob held a black marker, coloring the same picture he'd been working on for the past two hours—a circle drawn in black with a silver cat inside. Ruby stepped closer, noticing something over the cat's head. It looked like a hat, or a halo, but it was hard to tell. The cat's front paws were up, claws extended, like he was pushing against the circle, scratching, or trying to get out.

The child had an active imagination.

He always had.

The dozens of pictures she'd taped to her refrigerator over the past several months proved it.

An idea formed, a sort of potential loophole, and Ruby left Jacob for a moment and walked to the spare bedroom. She pulled a cardboard box from the top of the closet, which contained several toys Evie had played with when she was a child. The toy Ruby wanted was right at the top. She pulled it out, brushing a hand up and down its exterior. It had been so long since she'd been through the box she wasn't sure the toy still worked anymore. She tested it out, smiling when it sparked to life.

"Yes, yes," she said aloud. "This will do just fine."

When Ruby returned to the room, Jacob put the marker down, his eyes fixed on what she was holding in her arms.

She sat beside him, pointing at the picture he'd been drawing. "Is this for me?"

He nodded.

"It's a wonderful drawing," she said. "What is it?"

He took his eyes off the toy for a moment and looked up at her, his face vacant, and she bit down on her lip, willing herself not to cry. It was difficult seeing him in such a state. Something needed to be done.

She set the stuffed koala on the table and said, "Would you like to play with him?"

Jacob nodded.

"This koala was your mother's," Ruby said. "She never played with him much, though. She never liked stuffed toys or dolls. She preferred the outdoors, building things out of sticks and rocks. Most days, her clothes were filthy after she'd spent hours outside, searching for lizards or digging for bugs. Did you know your mother was like that when she was a child?"

He shook his head.

"Well, I bet your mom would have wanted you to have her toys," she said. "Would you like this one?"

Jacob nodded.

"Here, I want to show you something he does. Something special. He talks."

The koala came to life, saying his name was Kaspar the Koala. Then he asked if Jacob wanted to hear a story.

"Let's see, then," Ruby said. "I'll tell the first story, and then we'll let Kaspar tell the second. All right?"

Jacob offered a slight smile.

"One night, a mother gave her daughter a kiss and tucked her into bed," she began. "When she left the room, the little girl couldn't sleep. She knew she wasn't supposed to get out of bed, but she could hear her mother talking to a man in the living room. The little girl wanted to know who the man was and why he was at her house so late at night. She got out of bed, tiptoed to the door, and peeked out. And do you know what she saw?"

Jacob shook his head.

"She saw a man she'd never seen before," Ruby said. "A bad man. She knew he was bad because the man said mean things to her mother, and the little girl didn't like it. She wanted the man to go away, so she stepped out of her room. The man saw the little girl. He smiled at her and told her everything was going to be all right. Then he told her to go back to bed and not come out until her mother said it was all right. The little girl didn't want to go back to bed, though. She wanted to tell someone about the bad man in the house, but she was too frightened. She did what the man asked, getting back on her bed, grabbing her teddy bear, and holding him tight. She told the teddy bear everything she'd seen. When she was finished, she felt a lot better. And when she looked out her bedroom door again, the man was gone."

Ruby held the koala out toward Jacob. "Go on, Jacob. Kaspar is safe. You can tell him anything."

Jacob brought his knees to his chest and flattened his hands over his face.

From the entry way, she heard someone say, "Ruby? Are you here? The door was already open so I—"

Ruby's eyes widened, several swear words crossing her mind as Quinn entered the room. She looked at the koala and then at Jacob, before returning her gaze to Quinn.

Hands on hips, Quinn said, "What's going on here?"

"I was just showing Jacob some of Evie's old toys."

Quinn walked over to Jacob and gave him a hug. "Just stopping by to check in on you, sweetie. I need to speak to your grandma in the kitchen for a moment. I'll be right back, okay?"

He nodded, and Ruby and Quinn walked out of the room, neither of them saying a word until they reached the kitchen.

Ruby lifted a finger. "Before you say anything, Quinn, I'm not sure what you heard but—"

"You promised me you wouldn't push him before he was ready," Quinn said.

"I didn't. Nothing happened."

"But you were trying to *make* something happen, weren't you? Don't deny it. I know what I saw."

Ruby clamped her mouth shut, refusing to answer. Then something unexpected happened, sending both of them rushing back to the living room, their eyes on Jacob. He had placed the koala in front of him on the table, and with a hand cupped to the side of his mouth, he whispered, "I hid when the man in the mask hurt Mommy."

Jacob plugged his ears with his fingers and closed his eyes. Several seconds passed before they open again. He grabbed the koala, shaped his thumb and pointer finger into a gun, and said, "Pkurrr. Pkurrr."

22

Ruby rushed back to the kitchen, where she wasted no time phoning the police. Her action had caught Quinn off guard. She'd assumed Ruby wouldn't want to spoil the opportunity to keep Jacob talking. And by the time she was off the call, he'd clammed back up and returned to drawing, his new koala friend watching from his lap.

"You need to understand," Ruby started. "I was only trying to—"

"It might be best if we talked more about this later, Ruby, when we're alone," Quinn whispered.

Ruby shook her head. "And I say we take advantage of the fact that he's begun to speak. I'll bet he saw what happened, the little dear. As hard as it must have been on him, if he can ID the bastard, why not coax him a bit?"

"I disagree. We need to be careful. Jacob's going through a lot right now."

Ruby eyed Quinn with a look of disdain. "I like you, Quinn, but I think I know what's best for my grandson. *I'm* his family."

"I know you are, and I'm trying to respect your wishes. At the same time, we need to respect what he needs. It's important we go about this in the healthiest way possible. He may not be saying much right now, but in the past, he talked nonstop. Remember?"

"Yeah, yeah. Maybe you're right. What do you propose we do then?"

"I spoke with Edward McCallister earlier today. Quinn left me a letter."

"Oh? What did it say?"

"I haven't read it yet, but I know that in the event Roman and Evie both died, she wanted me to have custody of Jacob."

Ruby stepped back, gripping the edge of the counter as if she needed to keep herself from falling straight to the floor.

"I'm sorry," Quinn said. "I am not telling you this to upset you. I want Jacob to be in your life as much as he can. Whatever comes next, let's agree to work together."

There was a long pause, then she said, "How do you suggest we start?"

"I'd like Jacob to see a therapist."

Ruby started to respond, but then her attention switched to Jacob, who had just walked into the kitchen, yawning and rubbing his eyes.

"Are you tired, sweetie?" Ruby asked.

He nodded.

"Come along, then. I'll put a cartoon on for you, and you can get some rest in my room. How does that sound?"

She reached for his hand, and he took it, turning to wave at Quinn as they walked down the hall.

Once he was settled in, there was a knock at the front door. Quinn opened it, and Bo walked in with someone unexpected at his side. Kyle Grady.

Kyle offered her a wide grin and said, "Well, well, if it isn't Quinn Montgomery. I was hoping to run into you."

"Good to see you, Kyle," she said, smiling. "Since you're here with Bo, I'm guessing you're a detective now too?"

"Sure am."

Kyle was the same age as Quinn, and they'd gone to high school together. There was a time she'd considered dating him, but then she met Bo, and everything changed.

Kyle walked toward Quinn, scooping her into his muscular arms as he twirled her around. "Man, it seems like forever since I saw you last. We've missed you around here. How long you going to be in town?"

"Oh, I don't know. I've been thinking of sticking around."

"For good, you mean?"

"I think so."

"Well, that's great news."

Bo glanced at Kyle, his expression less than enthusiastic.

Kyle was quick to pick up on it, and he said, "What's the matter, Bo?"

"Nothing. I'm fine."

"You sure about that?"

"Yep."

"You wouldn't be bothered by me giving Quinn a little 'welcome back' hug, would ya? You're with Simone now."

Simone?

Who is Simone?

Earlier, when Quinn had seen Bo's father, he made no mention of Bo being in a relationship. Was there a secret girlfriend, one Bo hadn't brought around his family yet? Hearing he might be dating someone shouldn't have affected Quinn, but standing beside him now, it did, and she couldn't deny it.

Quinn had assumed Bo was single, and why wouldn't she? He'd gone through a lot of effort to talk to her in recent days. And when she'd stopped by his house, she saw no photos of him with another woman, no women's jacket on the coatrack, nothing to suggest he had a girlfriend.

It wasn't her place to ask, but she found herself blurting out, "Who's Simone?"

Bo gave Kyle a disappointed look, like he'd broken guy code.

Kyle placed a hand on Bo's shoulder and said, "My bad, man. You told me you've seen Quinn a few times. I figured she knew about Simone."

Bo deflected the conversation by changing the topic. "Where's Jacob?"

"He's watching cartoons in Ruby's bedroom," Quinn said. "Let's talk in the living room."

The two men nodded, following Quinn."

"Ruby called the police department, saying something about a picture he'd drawn," Bo said.

Quinn nodded, then looked around. "Yeah, I could have sworn the picture was on the coffee table before you two got here. I'm not sure what happened to it. I'll ask Ruby."

"What can you tell us about it?"

"It looked like he drew a cat with a halo over its head. I'm not sure it has anything to do with Evie's murder. He draws animals all the time."

"She also mentioned Jacob had spoken again."

"Yeah, not to us, but to Kaspar the Koala," Quinn said.

"Kaspar the ... what?"

"It's a stuffed koala Ruby got in Australia when Evie was a kid. Evie never had much interest in it, but she showed it to me once, and I thought it was cool. It's talks, tells stories and stuff."

"Oh ... kayyy. What did Jacob say?"

"He mentioned a man in a mask, and then he shaped his hand into a gun and made a sound like gunshots going off."

Bo rubbed a hand along his chin, thinking. "Let's say the

person Jacob saw, *if* he saw someone that night, murdered Evie. Even if they were wearing a mask, it's possible Jacob picked up on other details."

"Yes, he may have."

She knew where this was going.

"It would be great if he could tell us more about what happened that night. It's just ... I hate to have to put him through it."

Ruby entered the room and said, "Quinn thinks Jacob should see a therapist. After giving it some thought, I'm inclined to agree with her. Maybe a therapist would be able to get more details out of him in a way that makes him feel safe."

"Sounds like a good idea to me," Bo said.

Quinn turned toward Ruby. "What happened to the picture Jacob drew?"

Ruby glanced around. The markers were still there, but the picture was gone. "I have no idea, and Jacob's asleep. We can ask him about it when he wakes up."

"When you find it, text me a photo, all right?" Bo asked.

"Will do," Quinn said.

"We're chasing up a few leads," Kyle said. "I'd like to think we have a shot at nabbing this guy without putting Jacob through any more trauma."

"What leads?" Ruby asked.

"We can't talk about them right now," Bo said.

"Of course not," Ruby said. "You can't *talk* about anything."

"Ruby, please. We're doing our best."

"When you catch Evie's killer, *then* you'll be doing your best. Until then, I'm not so sure."

Bo shook his head. "We best get going. Before we leave, is there anything else we should know?"

"I can't think of anything," Quinn said.

"Call me if you do."

The four of them walked toward the front door, and Kyle turned toward Quinn. "Hey, I was just wondering, and it's okay to say no if you're not up to it, or if you're not interested. Do you have any dinner plans tonight?"

"I don't. I've been focusing as much of my energy as I can on Jacob."

"I'm off work in an hour. You wanna grab dinner with me? It would be nice to catch up with an old friend."

"Don't you think you're putting her on the spot, Kyle?" Bo cut in. "Evie just died, and Quinn's dealing with a lot right now."

"It's fine," she said. "Let me think about it. I'm not saying no, but I need to get Jacob settled first."

"He can stay here," Ruby said.

Quinn raised a brow. "I appreciate the offer. I just don't know if ..."

"Come on, Quinn. He'll be fine. We were just making plans to raise him together, right? Why not start now?"

When it came to trusting others, Quinn had always struggled. The idea of Ruby being alone with Jacob made her nervous. But Ruby was right. If they were going to try to raise him together, she had to come around to the idea that her way of raising him wasn't always going to mesh with Ruby's. They were going to have to find a way to work together for him above all else.

"All right, I'm going to head back to my parents' house," Quinn said.

She wanted nothing more than to go home, slip into a pair of flannel pajamas, crawl into bed, and unwind. But Kyle was a talker, and unlike Bo, Kyle was the type of person Quinn believed would give her details about where they were in their investigation.

"Tell you what," Kyle said, holding out his cell phone. "Put your number in here, and when I finish work, I'll give you a call. If you feel like getting out, we'll grab some burgers in town. If not, maybe we can get together some other time, when you're feeling more up to it. No pressure. I mean it."

23

"So, what's the deal with you and Bo ... if you don't mind me asking," Kyle said. "Seems like you two have some unresolved issues. Am I right?"

The first thing Quinn noticed after Kyle posed the question was his wandering eyes. He was trying his best not to stare at her chest but was failing. In the ten minutes since they'd been seated at Burger Bonfire, his attention kept darting back and forth—face, window, chest, like a fly trying to decide on a landing spot.

In part, she blamed herself. She'd worn a canary blue, low-cut, V-neck sweater. When she'd changed into it before he picked her up for dinner, it felt fine, and it looked fine ... at first. As the minutes ticked by, the shirt kept dipping lower, and she kept yanking it back up. She hoped she wasn't giving him the wrong impression, that said she'd worn the cleavage-revealing sweater on purpose, with him in mind.

"There is no *deal* between Bo and me," Quinn responded.

"You sure about that?"

Kyle cupped a hand around his triple-decker burger and

took a big bite, wiping his mouth with a napkin. "Can I ask a personal question?"

"I guess it depends on the question."

"Do you still have feelings for Bo?"

First Bo's father, and now Kyle.

"I ... I haven't told a lot of people this, but I'm going through a divorce," she said. "As far as my feelings for Bo are concerned, I don't have time to think about it right now."

She hoped the admission would be enough to shift the focus elsewhere.

"Did you mean it earlier when you said you're going to stay in town for a while?" he asked.

"I did. Being here feels right. I want to know what happened to Evie and why. It feels like I'm in limbo. I don't think I can move on with my own life until her murder is solved."

"I hear you. We're doing everything we can."

"I know you are."

"So, Quinn ... have you ever thought ... well, if the timing was different, that the two of us might have been a good match?"

"I've never given it much thought."

She felt bad after blurting it out, knowing he'd asked for a reason.

"Sometimes I think the right person could be sitting in front of you, and we don't even see it," he said as he laughed, shooting her a teasing wink.

"Right in front of me—meaning *you*?" she asked.

"Sure. Why not?"

"If I've given you the wrong impression by agreeing to meet for dinner tonight, I didn't mean to, Kyle. It's been great seeing you. But the truth is, what I just said is true. Between the divorce, Evie's murder, and how Jacob's taking it all, it's been a lot. I was hoping we could talk about other things, like Evie's case and what you know so far."

Kyle slid the burger back onto the plate and nodded. "Ah, the truth, at last."

"I'm having a good time with you, which is also the truth. It's nice to be here together, as friends."

"Friends, huh? Hey, I'm sorry if I made it awkward by making it about me just now. I should have been more sensitive about how you're feeling. When I saw you earlier today, I thought it was a shame we didn't hang out more in high school."

Quinn's face felt hot, her palms sweaty. "We didn't because you always had a girlfriend."

"As I recall, you had eyes for one person, and it wasn't me. And hey, it's okay. I'm glad we're friends."

Attempting to alter the course of the conversation, Quinn said, "Tell me about your life after high school. Any serious relationships?"

"Nope, I've never been married, even though I always thought I would be by now. I was engaged once to a woman named Skylar."

"When?"

"A couple of years after graduation."

"What happened?" Quinn asked.

"A few months before the wedding, she panicked and said she couldn't marry me."

"Did she say why?"

He reached for his glass, tapped a few pieces of ice into his mouth, and crunched down. "Skylar never wanted the marriage in the first place. She claimed she loved me, but she loved the idea of a career more. She didn't want kids, and I did. There was plenty of love there. We just couldn't manage to get on the same page."

"I'm sorry."

"Don't be. It was for the best. I was young, and so was she. If we had married, I doubt it would have lasted. I didn't see it then, but I do now."

He glanced out the window, expression downcast, like even though enough time had passed, the sting of Skylar's rejection still haunted him.

"Do you like being a police officer?" Quinn asked.

"It's a good job. I'd say I like it most of the time. Except ..." He blew out a long, hard sigh. "Finding Evie the way we did ... I've never seen anything like that before. I mean, I know things like this happen. I just didn't know it would happen to someone like her, someone I've known since we were kids. I wasn't prepared for it."

"None of us were."

He crossed his arms on top of the table, lowered his voice, and leaned in. "Wanna know something?"

"Sure."

"I can't sleep," he said. "Been having nightmares almost every night since it happened."

It wasn't the juicy bit of gossip she was hoping for, but she appreciated the vulnerability.

"I've been having nightmares too," she said.

"Evie wasn't just another girl I knew. She was one of us. This isn't a big town. Odds are someone we both know did this to her. You ever thought about it like that?"

"Every day since I returned. I feel like I don't look at people in this town the same way anymore. It's not fair, but I can't help how I feel. Everyone's a suspect."

"Tell me about it. You think it'll ever go back to the way it was before, and we'll all be able to get over it one day and move on?"

"I don't know," Quinn said. "This is a good town, filled with good people. It doesn't seem fair to allow one bad seed to change things. Maybe if we all knew what happened, if we knew the truth, we could heal. I've tried talking to Bo about what's going on in the investigation. You saw how he was at Ruby's. He won't tell me or anyone else anything."

"He tends to do things by the book. I mean, I admire him for it. This is a bit of a different situation, though."

Bo had always been a good guy, a rule follower, always trying to do what was right. She admired him for it too, even though it drove her crazy at times.

"I've been feeling so restless," Quinn said. "I can't sit around and do nothing. I need to stay active. I feel like if I don't, I'll lose my mind."

Kyle twisted his glass around in his hand, nodding. "I don't agree with Bo's decision to keep you out of the loop. With some things, sure, but not everything. I know what Evie meant to you, and I know how I'd feel if it was my friend. But I don't much like the idea of you running around trying to solve this on your own. And don't try and tell me it's not what you're doing either."

"I won't deny it. I want answers just like everyone else."

"Snooping around on your own ... it's not smart, Quinn. It's dangerous."

Her quest to gather information was going nowhere, and her thoughts turned elsewhere, to Jacob, and whether she should check in with Ruby.

"I'm tired," Quinn said. "This entire past week has been exhausting. Let's call it a night, okay?"

As she stood, he reached out a hand, catching her arm. "Oh, hell. Come on now. I didn't mean to offend you by suggesting you shouldn't try and find out what happened to Evie. If you sit back down, I'll answer what I can. Okay?"

Quinn paused a moment and then sat back down. "I know

the basics about what happened to Evie, the things everyone knows. If you don't mind saying, who are you talking to and who's a suspect?"

Kyle removed his baseball cap and scratched the back of his head. "This won't be what you want to hear, but okay. We're talking to everyone, looking at everyone—male, female, you name it. We're following every lead, even though right now, there's a lot we're still trying to piece together."

"What about the crime scene? What can you tell me about it?"

Kyle shook his head. "Trust me, Quinn. You don't want to know."

"Please, I ... the more I think about it, the more I recreate what happened in my mind—because I don't know what happened. I feel like I'm going crazy."

"If I tell you, and you can't handle it, I'll feel awful."

"I *can* handle it. Try me."

He blinked at Quinn, starting at her for a time before speaking again.

"What I'm about to tell you, I need it to stay with us," he said. "I don't need Bo flipping out on me because I shared private details with you."

"Yeah, sure."

Kyle waved the waitress over, a tall woman with a round face and braces. He ordered two coffees. The waitress shuffled away, and when she was out of earshot, he spoke again. "Ruby was the one who found them both. She'd stopped by to pick up Jacob and drive him to preschool, and she found him sitting on the bathroom floor, his clothes all stained and bloody. And Evie was right, you know ... there."

The visual hit Quinn hard, and a tear slid down her cheek. She flicked it away. "I can't imagine what it must have been like for him, sitting with his mother all night, alone."

"I try not to think about it. I arrived at Evie's house about the same time as Bo. Evie had been shot twice, both times in the head." Kyle leaned back, putting his ballcap back on. "I'm sorry, Quinn. It doesn't seem right telling you this stuff. You say you can handle it, but from where I'm sitting, I can see how hard it is on you."

"You're right, and maybe I'm not fine, but I still want to hear it."

Another pause and then, "We don't know if the killer was in the house before Evie got in the tub or whether he came in after. There were no signs of a struggle. As far as we can tell, she was taken by surprise."

"What about the house? Was anything missing or out of place?"

"We don't think so. As far as motives go, I'd guess it was personal. She had a bunch of cash on her dresser. If it was a robbery, seems the money would have been taken. Like I said before, we're looking at everyone ... the boyfriend, coworkers, clients who may have had a grievance. So far, it seems everyone loved her. No ill will anywhere."

"You also suspected Roman, didn't you?"

"About Roman ... yeah, we talked to him a few times."

"You found a shoe print that was a match to one of his shoes, right?"

"Right."

"He was at her house all the time, though," Quinn said. "What did he have to say about it?"

"He'd visited her on the day she died. They talked outside while she weeded her flowerbed. Seemed like a believable story. I mean, I've known Roman as long as you have, but I believed it."

"Did you search his house?"

"We did."

"Did you find anything?"

"Nothing unusual," he said. "Except the obvious."

"The *obvious*?"

"It seemed to me like he still loved his wife. He had a couple pictures of her lying around. There was also a photo of Roman, Evie, and Jacob stuck to the fridge."

The waitress returned, setting the coffees on the table. Then she turned, whistling as she trotted away.

"I talked with Roman before he died," Quinn said. "He told me he didn't have anything to do with what happened. I believe him."

Up to now, Kyle had held her gaze. When his eyes flashed to his coffee cup, it was unusual, like he was hiding something.

"What is it?" Quinn asked. "What aren't you telling me?"

"I don't believe Roman had anything to do with Evie's death, either. I've known him for a long time, frequented his bar once or twice a week. I've seen him at his best, seen him at his worst. He may not have been much of a talker, but he never struck me as the violent type or the kind of guy who'd murder his ex-wife, let alone the mother of his child."

"What about the rumors going around town about him? How did they get started?"

There was another pause, this time longer. "Rumors have a way of leading people in a general direction, kind of like cattle. Sometimes a well-planted rumor can be a good option."

A well-planted rumor?

What was he ...

"What are you getting at?" she asked.

"Say you need a diversion, something to make people think one thing while you concentrate on another. What I'm saying is, we wanted the public to believe we had a suspect, someone we were looking at for Evie's murder."

"Why?"

"As far as evidence goes, the crime scene was clean. We couldn't get Evie's boy to talk, and no one has come forward to say they saw anything or heard anything significant. We felt like we were at a dead end, so we sat down with the sheriff, and we came up with a new strategy."

Quinn shook her head, tapping a finger to the side of her coffee mug. "Are you saying your strategy was to make everyone believe Roman did it?"

"In a way. We wanted to point the public in the wrong direction. The killer might feel like he was in the clear and relax enough to slip up."

"I guess you all didn't factor in the effect it would have on Roman."

"Roman's death was an accident, Quinn. The guy was overwhelmed. It's not our fault."

"Whether it was or it wasn't, it was wrong." She stood. "I ... I need to go. Take me home, please."

She exited the restaurant, realizing she'd misjudged herself. Kyle was right. Talking about Evie's murder had been a lot harder than she realized. So hard she felt nauseous. As she made her way to the car, she heard footsteps, someone sprinting in her direction.

"Quinn ... wait," Kyle said. "I don't want you leaving here tonight thinking we set Roman up."

She whipped around, eyes like daggers as she looked at him. "Didn't you?"

"We didn't. Listen, Roman was in on the whole thing. It was *his* idea."

24

Twenty minutes later, Quinn stepped out of Kyle's car, the chill of the wind stinging her cheeks as she embraced the cool night air. She clutched what minimal warmth her thin denim jacket offered, pulling it close. As she started for the door, a noise rang out. It was close by. Quinn passed it off as nothing more than a piece of litter clanging down the empty street at first. Upon giving it more thought, she decided it had to be something else. The sound had been distinct, a jangle, like someone had dropped their keys.

She surveyed the area.

Her parents' house was dark.

So were most of the others in the immediate vicinity.

No one else was around.

Or were they?

She stood still for a moment, waiting, maybe even hoping she'd hear something again—home in on the exact location of the noise. But the night's wind had softened, and her surroundings went quiet.

A scent wafted past, an aromatic mixture of cedar and

citrus, one she recognized.

"You can come out from wherever you're hiding," she said. "I know you're there."

Bo stepped out of the shadows, his hands stuffed inside his coat pockets. "How'd you know it was me?"

She turned, walking toward the casita. "Your cologne gave you away."

"Can we talk?"

"I'm exhausted. Can it wait until morning?"

"I'm worried about you. I know you're out there sleuthing on your own, and dang it, Quinn … you're going to get hurt."

"I want to know what happened, as does everyone else. Are you saying everyone's in danger because they're curious?"

"What I'm saying is … if you keep digging like you are, and the wrong person gets wind of it, you could end up—" He stopped, as if he couldn't say the word.

"Dead? Like Evie?"

"I'm just saying you need to be careful."

"I'm taking precautions."

Quinn unzipped her handbag and lifted something out just far enough for Bo to see.

He took one look and shook his head.

"Where did you get the gun?" he asked.

"It was Evie's. It was hidden in her house, but I knew where she kept it."

"Hidden where? We did a full sweep, inside and out."

"Beneath a floorboard in her closet."

"Is it loaded?"

Quinn nodded.

"Lemme take a look at it," he said.

"Will you promise to give it back?"

"I will."

Quinn handed him the gun, and Bo looked it over. True to his word, he gave it back.

"Why did you want to look at it?" she asked.

"I needed to be sure it wasn't the gun used in her murder," he said. "It's not. But look, you can't run around town like a vigilante, Quinn. This isn't your fight."

She sighed, then walked to the door, entering the code to unlock it.

"I saw Kyle drop you off," Bo said. "Are you ... uhh ... I mean, it wasn't a date, was it?"

"We were two friends catching up on our lives."

"Do you plan on seeing him again?"

It was a bold question, and she was surprised he'd asked it.

"I might," she said. "Does Simone know you're here?"

He went quiet, which answered the question.

Simone didn't know.

"I appreciate your concern for my safety, but I'm all right," she said. "I can look after myself."

"Just a second, okay? Hang on ..."

Bo shoved a hand into his pocket and pulled out a small paper sack.

"What's that?" she asked.

"Hold out your hand."

She hesitated at first, then did as he requested.

He placed the sack into her palm, closed her fingers around it, and backed away. "I came here tonight to give you that, something I thought you'd like to have. Goodnight, Quinn."

25

Kyle tossed his car keys into a metal bowl and leaned against the kitchen cabinets, thinking about his dinner with Quinn. It had been difficult seeing how much pain she was in, a pain he knew all too well. The news of her divorce had him thinking about the past, about the way things had ended with his former fiancée.

The mention of Skylar's name triggered emotions from his past, ones he didn't like reliving. Everything he'd said at dinner was true … but he'd held back, just as Quinn had about discussing the end of her relationship.

There were things too hard to admit, things he was embarrassed about, ugly truths he didn't want to vocalize. Truths like him catching Skylar cheating on him with another man. As if that wasn't enough, he'd discovered she hadn't cheated just once during their relationship. She'd cheated twice.

As painful as it was when he discovered her deception, he still loved her, so he'd given her an ultimatum.

No more affairs, or it was over.

He thought she would agree to fight for their relationship.

After all, she said she still loved him.

Turned out, she didn't. Not enough.

Two days later, Skylar moved out of the apartment they shared, her rejection leaving him devastated and frustrated.

The one woman he loved had refused to put him first.

Every other woman he'd ever dated made him a priority.

Why couldn't she?

To relieve himself from feeling that kind of crushing pain again, he'd decided to remain a bachelor. In the years that followed, the lifestyle suited him, though in such a small town, it wasn't always easy finding women to date. Seeing Quinn today stirred up feelings he hadn't felt in a long time, shattering his personal belief that all women were the same.

There wasn't anything "same" about Quinn Montgomery.

She was kind, honest, real, and intoxicating. Given the chance, he believed he could develop feelings for her—real feelings—*if* she could ever like him enough to see him as someone more than a friend.

He wasn't sure she could.

But maybe one day ... one day when life wasn't as difficult for her as it was now, he'd get his chance.

26

The paper sack from Bo was resting on the nightstand, the same place it had been sitting ever since Quinn placed it there an hour earlier. Uptight about what the sack might contain, she wasn't ready to peek inside—not yet.

Leaning against the headboard of the bed, she shifted her attention, running her fingertips across the sealed envelope Edward McCallister had given her. She stared at it for several minutes, listening to the hypnotic tick of the clock on the wall.

She had something Evie didn't—time.

Still, her curiosity began to get the better of her, and she took a deep breath in and opened the envelope. Reaching a hand inside, she was surprised when she pulled out not one letter, but two. The first was addressed to her—the second to Jacob. She put Jacob's to the side, unfolded hers, and began to read.

Quinn,

I remember the first time I saw you, on your knees at the park with your disheveled hair and matching ribbons, your eyes stained with tears, face like a timid cat, afraid of everyone and everything. We were so different. Opposites. I never thought we'd end up the kind of friends we've become. But thinking back, I can see now why I befriended you that day and why a friendship with you was so appealing to me.

Looking into your big, round doe eyes was like looking into your soul. I saw all the qualities I lacked. All I could think about was if I hung around you long enough, maybe I'd get lucky and a part of you would rub off on me. And you know something, I believe it did. Because of you, I'm a softer, gentler person. Well ... I try to be, anyway. What's life without a bit of snark?

I bet you're sitting there right now, shaking your head, having a hard time believing I took the time to write this letter. Well, I did. And you have Harold to thank for it. I went in to discuss the future of my business, and somehow it turned into all of this—a will, a guardianship plan—the whole kitten caboodle (or is it kit and caboodle ... who knows!).

It feels a bit weird writing a letter I know you'll only ever read if I'm dead. It feels like I'm planning my own funeral, like I'm preparing to die. Death. I can't even imagine it at our age. Can you? Where do we go when we're nothing but a pile of ash?

Odds are you'll never even see this letter, but just in case you do, there are a few things I want you to know. For starters, I'm leaving you my business. Ha! How do you like that for an after-death shocker? I know, I know. Your gardening thumb is more black than green, but you're smart. I know you'll make sure what I worked so hard to create lives on without me.

I suppose there's not much chance Roman and I will both kick the bucket at the same time, making you Jacob's legal guardian. Still, Roman will need help, your help, and my son will need a strong woman to guide him. He has Ruby, but she won't be around forever. Look in on Roman now and then, would you? We may be apart, but I'll always love him, just like you'll always love Bo. And before you roll your eyes, be honest with yourself. You know I'm right.

To wrap things up, I just want to say one last thing. I love you.

You're a lot stronger than you realize. I know you're going to achieve great things, and I hope I'm around to see you do it. Okay, so that was two things. Suppose I'll be as defiant in death as I was in life.

All my love, my friend,

Evie

Quinn returned the letter to the envelope and managed a slight smile. She'd spent the day thinking that reading Evie's letter would only increase her sadness. But there was a level of comfort in Evie's words, a reminder that, although she was gone, Evie had lived her life her way, never compromising.

She set the letter to the side, tugged on the metal pull dangling from the lamp, and sat in darkness for a moment before tugging the light back on again. There was one more obstacle to get through if she expected to get any sleep.

She reached for the sack.

It felt weightless, like an inflated bag of air.

Removing the staple at the top, she pulled it free, taking in a deep breath as she looked inside, her eyes coming to rest on a familiar piece of shiny silver.

The last time she'd seen it, it had been dangling from Evie's neck.

27

Over the last five minutes, Quinn had pressed the call and end buttons on her cell phone three times, second-guessing, tapping the end-call button before the call had the chance to go through.

What if he didn't answer?

What if he answered and then hung up?

What if he said he didn't want to talk to her?

What if Simone answered?

What if!

She'd grown weary of "what-ifs."

She bit down on her bottom lip, pushed the call button again, and this time, she let it ring.

Bo's voice while groggy was upbeat when he answered, saying, "Hey, you."

"Hey, I'm sorry to be calling so late."

"Don't be. I'm glad you did."

"Are you with Simone? I wouldn't feel right talking to you right now if she's there."

"She's out of town, visiting her sister. And just to clarify, we're dating. We don't live together, and you shouldn't."

"I shouldn't what?"

"Feel weird about calling. Like you said, we're friends, right?"

Simone was out of town ... an interesting side note.

How would things change when she returned?

Would he keep stopping by?

Or would their daily communication come to an end?

"I feel like we keep going around in circles," Quinn said. "I don't want to argue with you."

"Let's agree not to then. Did you look inside the bag?"

"I did. How did you know the necklace would mean so much to me?"

"Before I was promoted to detective, I pulled Evie over one night for speeding. When I saw it was her, I asked about you. She said she'd tell me how you were if I promised not to give her a ticket."

Quinn laughed. "She sold me out to avoid paying a fine, eh? Nice."

"It worked. We got to talking, and she showed me the necklace. Then she told me about the day she got it. Knowing what it meant to both of you, I figured you'd like to have it."

"Am I to believe the straight-and-narrow detective just gave me something that should be in evidence?"

"I ... well ..."

"I'm teasing, Bo. It means so much that you brought it to me."

"Good."

"While I have you, when I went to see your dad today, he gave me a letter Evie had written to me, in the event of her, you know ..."

"I heard. What did it say?"

"Evie never planned on anything happening to her when she wrote it, of course, so it was more hypothetical than anything. She mentioned the business, looking after Jacob. She assumed if anything happened to her, he'd still have Roman."

"It's a shame. I liked Roman. He was a good guy."

"Kyle told me about the plan to convince the public Roman may have been involved in Evie's death."

Bo sighed. "Yeah, I feel awful about that now. He'll be exonerated one day, and everyone in the town will know the truth. You have my word on that."

"Even though they split up, Evie still cared about Roman."

"Well, yeah ... you know they were seeing each other again, right?"

The comment caught Quinn off guard.

"What do you mean?" she asked.

"Roman told me they were talking about getting back together."

"When?"

"Oh, about a week before she died, I'd say. I'm surprised you didn't know."

"Evie and I spoke a few times a week, at least. But right before she died, Marcus surprised me with an unexpected trip to Hawaii. We agreed to take our cell phones but not to use them much while we were gone. I'd called Evie before I left, and we were supposed to talk again the day I got back."

"Did Marcus and Evie get along?"

"They tolerated each other. He was jealous of her, though he'd never admit it. Whenever I stood up for myself, he blamed Evie. He believed she riled me up. He knew our marriage was faltering, and he blamed Evie for trying to break us up."

Bo went silent for a time. "Curious, don't you think?"

"What's curious?"

"Your husband didn't like Evie, and right before she died, he whisked you away on a vacation. That doesn't alarm you?"

A light went on in Quinn's head as she realized what he was getting at.

"Marcus isn't a killer," she said. "No way. Besides, there are other people you should be looking at."

"And who would that be, Nancy Drew?"

She let his wisecrack slide. "Evie's boyfriend, Ray Ferguson."

"We've questioned him twice. We also have him under surveillance."

"And?"

"There's no evidence to suggest he did it, not enough to hold him, anyway."

"If he found out Roman and Evie were talking about getting back together, there's your motive. Ray went to her house that night. What if it was to confront her about Roman, and in the heat of the moment, he murdered her?"

"Wait a minute. What night?"

"The night Evie was murdered," she said.

"Where are you getting your information?"

"Mrs. Healy."

Bo let out a long, frustrated sigh. "What time did she see Ray at Evie's?"

"She didn't."

"How can she be sure it was him, then?"

"She said she recognized Ray's headlights."

"Huh, I spoke to Mrs. Healy, and she didn't mention it."

"I get the impression she has a bit of a grudge against law enforcement."

"Ray told me the last time he saw Evie was the morning of her murder."

"Then he's lying," she said.

"Or Mrs. Healy is mistaken about what she saw."

"She seemed certain when she told me. Maybe you need to talk to Ray again."

"Maybe you're right."

28

A week had passed since Evie's death, but to Quinn, it seemed like a lifetime. Days bleeding together, one by one, until she couldn't even remember what day it was anymore. The headstone Ruby had chosen for Evie was a gray-speckled stone with rough edges. In the oval center was a picture of Evie, and below it the words: *Though absent you are always near, still loved, still missed, and oh so dear.* The rhyme Ruby selected was sweet, although nothing Evie would have chosen for herself. Evie would have appreciated something with a bit more sass, like a saying Quinn had once seen while touring an old cemetery: *Here lies Eddie Yeast, pardon me for not rising.*

Standing in front of her grave now, Quinn felt nothing.

No pain, no emotion.

Was it progress?

Or a sign she was going numb?

Or both?

She wasn't sure.

She clutched a wildflower bouquet in front of her, which she'd cut from Evie's garden that morning. She knelt, positioning the flowers in front of other floral arrangements that had been placed there on the day of the funeral.

Pressing a hand to her chest, she rolled her fingers over the chain of Evie's necklace and said, "Thanks for the letter, Evie. I miss you. We all do."

Quinn remained a little longer and then started for her car, stopping when she noticed a young woman walking toward Evie's grave. The girl was dressed in a mini skirt, puffy jacket, and a pair of thick, sheepskin boots. She was tall, on the slender side, and looked to be in her late teens. The girl placed the plant she was holding in front of Evie's headstone and then turned, blinking at Quinn.

"Hey," Quinn said.

"Hi," she said.

"Beautiful plant."

She shrugged. "I guess so. Rowdy asked me to bring it."

Rowdy?

"Who's Rowdy?" Quinn asked.

"He's a landscaper."

"Did he work for Evie?"

"Sure did."

"Shouldn't you be in school?"

"I'm a senior. I have work release. I work ... I mean to say, I worked for Evie. Well, I still work for her, but the thing is, none of us are sure about what's going to happen to the business now that she's gone. We're doing our best to keep it going, but ..."

"Do you like working there?"

"I love it. It's like art, you know? Working with plants, land-scaping a yard, making it beautiful. Being outside instead of cooped up behind a desk all day is the best."

"I saw you at Evie's funeral," Quinn said. "What's your name?"

"Marissa Lewis. What's yours?"

"Quinn Montgomery."

Marissa wagged a finger in the air. "Ah, I thought so. You and Evie were good friends."

"We were," Quinn said. "How long have you worked for her?"

"About six months. I'm worried that now she's gone, I might have to start looking for another job."

"Why?"

"I'm guessing the business will either close down, or be put up for sale, or someone else will step in. I'm not sure I want to work for anyone else. My plan was to learn all I could from Evie, and then one day, if she felt like retiring, I could take it over from her."

"You're not planning on going to college?"

"My mom and my stepdad expect me to, but no ... I have other plans, *big plans* with a certain someone. If I have my way, a year from now, I'll be married."

Marissa was too young to be considering marriage, in Quinns opinion—even though Quinn and Marcus had been about the same age when they'd married. Which was her point. But it wasn't her place to comment.

"I should have stopped by Evie's workplace sooner so I could meet everyone," I said. "I've just had a lot going on since I've been back in town. If it makes you feel better, the business isn't going to be closed, and it's not going to be sold. Not if I can help it."

"How can you be sure?"

"Because Evie left her landscaping business to me."

Marissa stepped back, looking surprised. "To *you*? Do you know anything about gardening and landscaping?"

"Not much, but I'm a quick learner, and I will do whatever it takes to see the company Evie started survives. Do you think

Evie's employees would be willing to meet with me tonight? I'd like to discuss the business, the clients, and get to know all of you."

"We've all been a little freaked out, waiting to find out what's going to happen. So yeah, I'm sure they'll all be interested to meet with you."

"What time do you close today?"

"Five o'clock."

"All right. Let's meet at the workplace at 5:30. I'll bring dinner."

"Great," Marissa said. "I'll round everyone up, and we'll see you then."

29

Ruby opened the front door, huffing a sigh as she stared at Quinn.

"Is everything all right?" Quinn asked. "You seem upset."

"The investigation into Evie's murder is going nowhere. Every time I talk to the police, they have nothing new to tell me."

"I'm sure they're doing all they can."

Ruby rolled her eyes, muttering something under her breath.

"I was wondering, have you found the picture Jacob drew yet?" Quinn asked.

"Yeah, and I have some bad news, I'm afraid. He crumpled it up and threw it into the trash. By the time I realized it, I'd already poured pasta sauce over it, and … well, it's ruined."

It wasn't the outcome Quinn had hoped for—or would have imagined.

"Can I come in?" she asked.

Ruby nodded and turned, waving her inside. "I'll put some coffee on."

Quinn entered the house and looked around. "Where's Jacob?"

Ruby pointed down the hall. "He's snuggled up in my bed watching cartoons."

"How has he been today?"

"Seems fine. Ate all his lunch, and he even cracked a little smile for me when I gave him a couple of chocolate chip cookies. He's going to be all right, you know. Maybe not today, and maybe not tomorrow, but he'll get there."

"You know to call me if he—"

"Says anything ... yes, yes. I'm well aware you'd like to stay updated, dear."

"I'm going to look in on him and say hello, okay?"

Ruby shrugged. "Suit yourself."

Quinn walked toward the bedroom, noticing the bedroom door was ajar when she got to it. She pushed it open and glanced inside, her eyes coming to rest on the bed.

Jacob *wasn't* there.

She flipped the light on, her eyes darting around.

"Ruby, I can't find him," Quinn shouted. "He's not in here."

"Not to worry. I'm sure he's here somewhere."

Quinn took a deep breath in, trying not to panic.

He was there.

Everything was fine.

There was no need to worry.

But worry, she did.

She crossed the hall, checking one of Ruby's guest rooms. The floor was littered with toys, but there was no sign of Jacob. In an instant, Quinn felt a sharp sting of regret. As the panic surrounding the boy's whereabouts mounted, it wasn't long before her mind went somewhere she didn't want it to go.

What if Jacob had been taken?

As she considered the possibility, she heard what sounded

like a toilet being flushed, the sloshing water echoing into the hallway. In her haste to find him, Quinn hadn't noticed the en suite bathroom door in Ruby's bedroom was closed.

Jacob tiptoed out, yawning as he rubbed his eye. "Hi, Winn."

Quinn ran to him, dropping to her knees as she pulled him into an embrace.

Ruby entered the room and smiled. "Like I said, he's here, and he's fine. I wouldn't let anything happen to him. I hope you believe me."

"I do," Quinn said. "I'm just a little on edge."

"Makes sense. We all are."

Jacob stared up at Quinn, and much to her surprise, he spoke. "I miss Mommy, Winn."

Quinn and Ruby shared a glance, and she ran a hand through his hair. "I know you do, sweetheart."

He yawned once more and walked over to the bed.

"He hasn't napped yet. I bet he's tired." Ruby tucked a blanket around his small frame and kissed him on the forehead. "Nanny's in the kitchen if you need anything."

He nodded, and Quinn followed Ruby to the table where two cups of coffee were waiting. Ruby reached into an open cabinet, removed a bottle of whiskey.

She shook the bottle, saying, "Care for a little something extra to top it off?"

"No, thank you."

"Don't mind if I have a little myself." Ruby poured a capful. "I see you looking at me with those hawk eyes of yours. I'm sober, and you know it. I'd never put our boy in jeopardy, not on my watch."

Our boy.

It was nice to be acknowledged.

For the next several minutes, they sipped their coffee, reminiscing on some of their favorite memories they'd shared with Evie.

"I want Jacob to be in your life as much as he can," Quinn said.

Ruby placed a hand over Quinn's. "I appreciate it. To tell you the truth, I think she made the right decision, picking you. I'm ... well, not as quick on my feet as I used to be. And besides, everyone can see how much the kiddo adores you. Did you come all the way over just to tell me that? You'd said as much last time you were here."

"I ... no. I wanted to apologize."

"Why?"

"I was a bit rough on you during my last visit. I'm just trying to do right by Jacob, and I know you are too. We both want what's best for him, and together, I know we'll give him a good life."

Ruby raised her glass. "I'll drink to that."

"While I'm here, I ... ahh, I wanted to ask you something."

"What's on your mind?"

"Ray Ferguson. What can you tell me about him?"

Ruby's expression soured. "Don't care for the man. He's a liar, for starters. I hear he told police he was amicable about the split with Evie. Said they both wanted it. Not true."

"Did Evie end things with Ray because she was thinking about going back to Roman?"

"In a way. Dating Ray made her realize how much she still cared for Roman. She decided it wasn't right, being in a relationship with a man while still having unresolved feelings for another."

"Did Ray know why she ended things?"

"Evie told him she wasn't ready to be in a serious relationship. But if you ask me, Ray knew there was more to it. He never liked Roman, and he didn't like the idea that they'd remained such good friends after the divorce."

"Mrs. Healy told me she saw Ray driving over to Evie's house the night of the murder. Ray told Bo he hadn't been there that night."

Ruby shook her head. "Norma Healy. Old coot. Mark my words, my money's on Ray. I think his jealousy got the better of him, and he killed her. And before you say anything else, you should know I've thought about it long and hard. The man is a leech. He hung around, spending her money like it was his own. I couldn't stand it."

"Evie wasn't the type of person to stay with a guy like that."

"He was charming and ... well, she had a soft spot for him. I never could understand why. Then again, she always had a soft spot for the wounded ones, always thought she could swoop in and fix them, I guess."

If Ruby was right, and Ray had murdered Evie, the motive could have been twofold. Anger over the breakup and no longer benefitting from Evie's money, and jealousy over her relationship with Roman. If he got wind that Evie and Roman were seeing each other again, it may have been enough to put him over the edge.

The more Quinn thought about it, the more she wanted to meet Ray, to assess him for herself.

"Have you spoken to the police about Ray?" Quinn asked.

"I have. They keep saying they're 'looking into it.' Feels like I'll go to the grave before they gather up enough evidence to convict the man. They're tailing him, but to what end, I do not know."

"How did you know Ray was under surveillance?"

Ruby screwed her face into a wry grin. "I have my ways. The police can't sit there forever. One day they'll move on, and when they do, Ray and I will have a little chat."

"Do you have a plan? Are you going to try and get him to confess?"

"I haven't decided yet. I have half a mind to kill the man and be done with it."

Ruby had laughed when she said it, but the look in her eye was telling. When it came to Ray, it seemed Ruby was considering her options. And Quinn got the sense that right now, the options were leaning in one direction.

30

Quinn lounged on her parents' front porch swing, dangling a leg over the side as she watched the door of Bo's truck swing closed. When she'd first returned to town, it had been hard seeing him, but now she welcomed his daily visits. She looked forward to them, even, and she wondered how long Simone would be away.

Bo walked up the porch steps and tipped his head toward Quinn, offering her a broad smile. "Good to see you."

"Good to see you too."

He stared at her for a time, then said, "Looks like you have something on your mind. Care to talk about it?"

"I had an interesting conversation with Ruby today. She's sure Ray is responsible for Evie's death. She even made a snide comment about offing him one day."

"Sounds like something Ruby would say. Do you think she was being serious?"

"She laughed after she'd said it, but when it comes to her, who knows?"

Bo pointed at the swing. "Mind if I sit?"

Quinn sat up and scooted over, making room.

Bo took a seat and turned toward her. "I know you have a lot of questions about Evie, and I haven't done a great job of communicating with you. I guess what I'm saying is ... maybe it would be best if I was more forthcoming with you."

"What are you saying?"

He shrugged. "I'm saying ... ask me whatever you like."

"Do you mean it?"

"I may not be able to tell you everything, but I'll tell you what I can. I just need anything I say to stay between us for now, all right?"

"Yeah, sure. What changed your mind?"

"I've been avoiding discussing the details of the investigation with you because I wanted to keep you safe. Now I think it might be better to keep you close. If I don't, I'm afraid you'll get yourself into trouble."

Quinn laughed. "You may be right."

"Oh, I *know* I'm right. I also don't want you going to Kyle for answers. He's been talking about the dinner you two had together all day. If you want to know something, I'd rather you ask me."

Was his real reason for offering to open up a way to keep her from seeing Kyle?

She assumed it was, in part, at least.

"I'd rather talk to you," she said. "As for Kyle, the dinner didn't last long, and he took me home after that."

Bo seemed pleased. "I'd like you to make me a promise. From now on, if you're thinking about talking to anyone who may be involved with Evie's murder, I want to know about it beforehand. Shoot me a text or give me a call. Okay?"

"Sounds reasonable."

"And one more thing. I need you to be honest with me."

"I have been."

"The gun you're packing around, do you know how to use it?"

"I've shot pop bottles with my dad since I was a teenager. I might be a little rusty, but my aim's decent."

Bo extended a hand in her direction. "Let's shake on our new agreement."

Quinn ignored the hand, throwing her arms around him instead. As soon as she did, she second-guessed herself, thinking the move had been a bad idea. He was seeing another woman. It wasn't right. But before she could break away, he wrapped his arms around her, holding her tight.

It felt good, being there in his arms.

It also felt wrong.

She pushed back.

"I'm sorry ... I shouldn't have," she said. "I didn't mean to—"

"You didn't do anything wrong. It's fine."

"Let's ... ahh, let's talk about Evie."

"What do you want to know?"

"When I talked to Kyle, he was careful about what he said, and even then, he didn't say much. But he did mention a shoe print. What can you tell me about it?"

"The print was found outside the home. Denstone was poured over the impression to see what details we could get from it."

"What's that?"

"It's a runny substance, looks like pancake batter. It hardens over the impression. Then it's taken to the forensics lab for analysis. It's a men's tennis shoe, size eleven."

"Do you know what size shoe Ray wears?"

"Depends on the shoe. Sometimes ten and a half, sometimes eleven. He let us into his house the first time we stopped by, and he didn't ask for a warrant either. Said he had nothing to hide. We checked his shoes. None of the soles were a match."

"No surprise there. If he's guilty, he would have gotten rid of the shoes, I'd guess." She paused, then said, "In the spirit of honesty, I've been thinking about going to Ray's place. I want to talk to him."

"I figured as much. Is there anything I can say to talk you out of it?"

"I have too many questions to let it go. If Ray lied about seeing Evie the day she died, he could be lying about a lot more."

Bo pressed his hands against his jeans and stood. "Care to find out if there's any truth to your theory?"

"Are you suggesting we talk to him together?"

"I am, because if we don't, I know you will, with or without me. And like I said before, I aim to keep you close."

31

Ray Ferguson lived in a single-wide trailer a few miles out of town. As Bo came to a stop on Ray's gravel driveway, two things caught Quinn's eye. First, a Doberman pinscher sleeping inside a rectangular patch of sunlight on the unfinished-wood porch. And second, a pickup truck parked in front of the trailer. The driver's-side door was open, and the truck's bed was packed, like someone preparing to leave.

Bo glanced at Quinn, seeming to notice her trepidation about the dog. "Hey, don't worry about Magnus. He's a barker, not a biter. Hasn't tried to bite me yet, anyway."

The trailer door opened, and a man stepped out.

In the looks department, he wasn't anything like Quinn had expected.

"That's *him*?" Quinn asked. "That's Ray?"

"In the flesh."

Ray was bald and buff, the kind of buff that made Quinn suspect his athletic physique been achieved from something more than just regular workouts at the gym.

"He's nothing like I thought he would be," Quinn said. "Evie had a type. Ever since we were teenagers, she's always dated the same kind of guy. This guy doesn't fit it."

"What was her type?"

"Tall, lanky, shaggy-haired, outcasts like Roman. In looks, Ray is the total opposite."

Ray was carrying a duffel bag, which he tossed into the truck's cab. Then he wiped his hands on his stained, ripped jeans and walked over.

Bo put the window down.

Ray folded his arms and leaned in, resting them on the sill.

"Do you need something, Detective?" Ray asked. "I thought we cleared everything up last time you were here."

Bo pointed at Ray's truck. "You goin' somewhere?"

"I sure am. I'm leaving town for a few days."

"When?"

"Stopped home to get a few things loaded on my lunch break so I can head out right after work."

"When will you be back?" Bo asked.

"What's it to you?"

"You know exactly what it is to me."

"And you know I've said all I have to say."

While a bit rough around the edges, Ray was handsome, even if he wasn't Evie's "type." There was a charm to him, a charm Quinn believed had drawn Evie in. The more he talked, the more she found herself hanging on to his every word. It made sense now why Evie had fallen for him.

Ray was someone different.

Someone new.

A change of scenery.

Ray glanced over at Quinn and grinned, his eyes focused on the chain hanging around her neck. "Nice necklace."

"I think so."

"You must be Quinn. Evie showed me pictures of you when she was ... when we dated."

Quinn forced a smile, trying to keep her cool as she shifted the topic of conversation. "Going anywhere fun?"

"Just a little road trip to Wendover. Boss gave me the next few days off. Been itching for a good poker game."

"Before you go, I have a few more questions," Bo said.

Ray swished a hand through the air. "Like I said, man, I'm done talking. Either arrest me or get off my property. That clear enough for you?"

"First off, this isn't *your* property. You're squatting on Max Howard's property. He may be your boss, but he's also a friend of mine. I have every right to be here."

Ray's trailer door opened a second time, and a woman with long, curly, blond hair stepped out. Given she had been a brunette in high school, it took a moment for Quinn to recognize her. The woman saw Bo's truck and halted, looking shocked to see Ray had a visitor.

She took one look at Bo and turned.

Quinn opened the door and hopped out, shouting, "Hello, Janae. It's been a while."

Janae whipped back, her eyes narrowing as they met Quinn's gaze. She descended the porch steps, the bottom of her long, low-cut maxi dress swishing across them as she walked toward Quinn. "Oh. My. Gosh. Quinn Montgomery. Is that you? I heard you were in town."

The dog jolted to a standing position, barking until Ray yelled a series of commands, silencing him.

Janae approached, and Quinn leaned in, whispering in her ear. "What are you doing with Ray?"

"We work together. Why?"

"You're aware he dated Evie, right?"

"Of course I am. I'm not trying to make a move on him. I'm married."

Janae lifted her hand, flashing a silver band with a tiny, pear-shaped diamond in the center.

"Why are you at Ray's house?" Quinn asked.

"We're on our lunch break. We ran out to pick up a couple of sandwiches. On our way back to work, he asked if we could stop by his house and load a few things for his trip this weekend. And ... well, here we are."

The story seemed legit.

But was it?

Janae was acting odd, almost like she was hiding something.

"You need to be careful," Quinn said.

Quinn had tried to whisper the warning, but when Ray jerked his head toward her, stopping the conversation he was having with Bo midsentence, she knew she'd failed.

"Be careful of what?" Ray asked. "Be careful of *me*?"

Quinn went quiet, trying to decide what to say next.

Playing nice was becoming too hard to keep up.

And why should she?

"You said the last time you saw Evie was on the morning of her murder," Quinn said.

"What about it?"

"Mrs. Healy saw your truck on the road to Evie's house the night she died."

He shrugged. "She's mistaken. If she saw a truck, it wasn't mine."

"Are you sure? You have a broken headlight, don't you?"

"Like I'm the only person in town who drives around with a busted light."

"I tell you what, let's gets Mrs. Healy in a room with you,

Ray, and we'll all sit down and go over what she saw that night," Bo said. "Keep in mind, she's an observant woman."

"An observant woman or a senile, old broad?" Ray said.

"Seemed plenty 'with it' to me when we talked. If I bring her in, and she can prove you're lying ... well, you know what comes next."

Ray threw his arms in the air and said, "All right, fine. I was at Evie's all of five minutes the night of the murder. Got in. Got out. She was alive when I left. I swear."

"What time?" Bo asked.

"Around eight thirty, I guess."

"Why did you lie to me the first time I questioned you?"

"I'm new here. Why do you think? You wouldn't have believed me, and I would have become an easy target. Don't tell me I'm wrong, because I'm not."

"What was your reason for stopping by Evie's house?" Quinn asked.

Ray hesitated, saying nothing.

Quinn turned toward Bo. "He just admitted he was at Quinn's house the night of the murder after lying about it before. What are you going to do about it?"

"Quinn ..." Bo started.

"See what I mean?" Ray said, head shaking. "It doesn't matter what I say. No one in this town is going to believe me."

"Answer the question," Bo said. "What were you doing at Evie's house?"

"I left my fishing gear at her house. I stopped by to get it because I had a trip planned with my buddies that weekend."

"Can anyone corroborate your story?"

"Yeah, a couple of my coworkers."

"Names?"

Janae raised a hand. "I was on the fishing trip."

"So, you can vouch for him the day *after* Evie's murder, but you don't know where he was on the night she died, correct?" Bo asked.

"I ... well, kinda," Janae said. "What I meant to say is, I stopped by his place to get a list of things I should pick up at the store for the trip. Beer, sandwiches, and snacks ... things like that."

"What time?"

"I dunno. Seven or eight."

"How long did you stay?"

"Maybe thirty minutes."

"Let me ask you this," Ray said. "If I was planning on murdering Evie, why would I tell my coworkers I was stopping by her house? Seems like a stupid thing to do if I was planning on killing her."

Quinn didn't want to admit it, but Ray was right.

It would have been a stupid thing to do.

"What was Evie doing when you arrived at her house?" Bo asked.

"She'd just given Jacob a bath. He was in his pajamas, in the living room, working on a new puzzle she bought him. Evie was in a robe, running water into the tub."

"The same tub she was found dead in," Quinn spat.

"You don't even know me," Ray said. "Innocent until *proven* guilty, and I'm *not* guilty."

Quinn felt her breath quickening, and she fisted her hands, wanting nothing more than to take her frustration out on Ray.

He'd lied before.

Was he lying now?

Bo looked at Quinn, lowering his voice as he said, "Can I talk to you for a minute?"

Quinn nodded, and glanced over at Ray and Janae. "You two, stay put. We'll be right back."

Bo and Quinn walked to the truck, and he opened the door, urging her to get in.

"I don't want to, Bo," she said. "I'll bet he's still lying. He's not going to get away with—"

"Please," he said. "I know what I'm doing. If it turns out he had anything to do with Quinn's murder, he'll pay for what he's done. Right now, I need you to trust me."

She huffed a frustrated sigh and then said, "All right."

She hopped into the cab, and Bo took out his phone, making a call. Then he walked back over to Ray and Janae. They talked for several more minutes, and a police car rolled up. Kyle hopped out of the passenger side, offering Quinn a smile and a wave as he approached Bo. The two spoke for a few minutes, and then Quinn heard Bo say, "Escort Ray and Janae back to work, and then question the coworkers who were supposed to have gone fishing with him. See if their stories match up."

Bo then turned to Ray. "You can forget about your trip to Wendover or wherever it was you were going."

"You can't tell me what I—" Ray started.

Bo stabbed a finger to the man's chest. "You've just admitted to giving me a false statement. Be glad I'm not arresting you right now. I'm going to have a chat with Mrs. Healy, and we'll go from there. For now, I want you to stick around. Try to leave town, and I'll have you arrested."

32

Quinn buried her head in her hands. "I don't like it, Bo."

His eyes left the road just long enough to glance her direction. "Don't like what?"

"The rumors circling around town still have a lot of people thinking Roman is to blame for Evie's death. It's not right. You're creating a false sense of security. What if he slips past those police officers?"

"By 'he' you mean Ray?"

"Ray just admitted he was at Evie's right before she died. If what Mrs. Healy's saying is true, Ray was the last person seen coming and going."

Bo pulled to a stop in front of Quinn's parents' house, and she hopped out of the truck.

"I'm going to talk to Mrs. Healy now," he said. "And before you ask, I'm not taking you with me this time. I want to see if she tells me the same story she told you."

While Quinn wanted nothing more than to tag along, she knew when to push and when to hold back.

"If you learn anything new, will you call me?" she asked.

"I'll tell you what I can. What are your plans for the night?"

"I'm meeting Evie's employees at their workplace, and then Ruby's dropping Jacob off. We're having a quiet night in."

"Good."

Quinn opened the truck door and stepped out.

"I doubt I'll get the chance to tell you about my visit with Mrs. Healy until tomorrow," he said. "Just didn't want you waiting up for my call."

"Sounds like you're the one with plans tonight."

"Simone's back in town. We're, ahh ... supposed to be getting together later."

Quinn thought of an aloof way to respond, to make it seem like his comment didn't affect her, but the words wouldn't come.

Say something.

Anything.

Don't just stand here.

"Yeah, okay," she said. "Have a good time on your date."

Have a good time on your date?

She felt like an idiot, like she supported the idea of him being in a relationship with someone else. She shut the truck door and sighed, hoping he'd drive away.

But he didn't leave.

He sat there, the truck idling as she walked toward the house.

She tried not to read too much into it at first, but as she reached the doorstep and glanced back, he was still there.

Why wasn't he leaving?

It didn't make sense.

Had he hoped she would say something other than what she had?

Her heart was beating faster now, and in a sudden moment of impulse, she pivoted, heading back to the truck.

Bo was staring straight ahead, his expression forlorn.

She knocked on the window, startling him.

The window came down, and he said, "Are you okay?"

"Are *you* okay?"

"I'm fine."

"Okay, then. I'll talk to you tomorrow."

She blew out a frustrated breath, knowing she'd made an even bigger fool of herself than she had before.

"Hang on a second," Bo said. "Is there something you want to say?"

There was a lot she wanted to say.

She just didn't know whether she dared say it.

"I was just wondering if you ... if you ... ahh ..."

"If I, what?" Bo pressed.

"I know you haven't dated Simone long, but do you ... umm, have feelings for her?" As soon as the words left her lips, she closed her eyes, feeling an immediate sense of regret. "Forget it. It's none of my business. I shouldn't have asked."

Bo tapped his thumb against the steering wheel. "Would it bother you if I did?"

"Do you?"

"I don't know, Quinn. You're putting me on the spot here."

"You're right. I'm sorry. I'm ... I'm gonna go."

He put the truck in gear and pulled away, and she stood there, watching the truck fade into the distance. Inside, her stomach was in knots, feeling a surge of unrest.

Only this time, it wasn't just for Evie.

33

Two Hours Later

Marissa Lewis hummed the tune of Blake Shelton's "Bringing Back the Sunshine," the rhythmic beat of her hot pink sneakers dancing their way down the asphalt street. She'd thought about driving to Quinn's work meeting, but unlike the early-morning chill she'd felt earlier, the sun was now beaming down on her. And, as if that wasn't enough, there was almost no wind. She hadn't seen a day this glorious in over three weeks, and with winter nudging its icy finger through fall's door, she wasn't about to pass up the opportunity for one last stream of sunshine.

It was hard to believe her last year of high school was in full swing, the days passing by like the turn of pages. At seventeen, she was the youngest student in her grade to graduate, thanks to skipping a grade a few years earlier. In eight months, she'd get her diploma, and then ...?

She had plans.

Big plans.

And they were all coming together with one exception—her career.

Evie was dead, and she was ... well, *screwed*, her opportunity to learn the landscaping business and slide into a better position at work dashed now that Quinn was taking over the place. Evie was no longer there to mentor her as she'd promised. She didn't see any way the business could survive without her.

"Bye, bye, high school, and *hello*, college dormitory," her mother had said to her during a recent conversation. "It will be here before you know it. Aren't you excited?"

Excited?

The thought of leaving town to endure even more years of school soured her stomach. She didn't want to go. She wanted to stay in Cody. She belonged here. And that's why she did what she knew she had to do—she came up with a back-up plan. A foolproof plan B. The future of her career may have been up in the air, but as far as she was concerned, she had a golden ticket to remain in Cody for good.

As she thought about the future, a vehicle with charcoal, matte-finish rolled alongside her, and she brought her eyes down from the sky.

The car lulled to a stop, and the passenger-side window lowered in what seemed like slow motion, the clumsy, hand-pumped cranking taking a lot longer than the electric-powered windows of modern cars.

"Hey, you need a ride?" the man asked.

She snickered, thumbing at his car, teasing him. "In that old thing?"

He ignored the question and said, "Oh, come on. This car's a classic, just got it out of the shop."

"I'm walking. It's good exercise. You should try it sometime."

"Where are you headed?" he asked.

"To a work meeting. I met Evie's friend Quinn today, found out she's taking over Evie's business. Evie left it to her."

"She ... *what*?"

"Imagine what Quinn will think, what they'll *all* think when they find out about us," she said under her breath. "Shock of a lifetime."

"What was that?" he asked.

"Oh, nothing."

"Where'd you meet Evie's friend?"

"I went to the cemetery to leave something on Evie's grave. Quinn was there, and we talked for a while."

"About work?"

Marissa shot him a wink. "And other stuff, girl talk. Anyway, I'm not excited about the meeting."

"Why not?"

"Quinn doesn't know anything about gardening and landscaping, I guess. Once Evie's clients find out, I doubt they'll stick around. I'm just bummed. Evie knew I didn't want to go to college, and she supported it. She was going to talk to my mom and my stepdad, try to help them see my passion for landscaping. Now she's dead, and everything's just ... screwed. *I'm* screwed."

She paused, curious to hear his reaction.

"Would college be such a bad thing?" he asked.

Marissa opened the passenger-side door and poked her head in, flashing a mischievous grin in his direction. "I don't know ... *would it*?"

"Not if you care about your education."

"Are you saying you *want* me to go?"

"I never said that," he said.

"What then?"

"Of course I'd rather keep you here."

She leaned across the front seat, her hot breath seducing his lips. "You know I'd miss you if I had to leave."

"How much?" he teased.

"A lot."

"Show me."

"Here? Someone might see us."

"Not here. Let's go somewhere else."

Marissa checked the time on her cell phone. "Can it wait until after the meeting?"

He reached out, caressing her arm. "She can wait."

Marissa leaned in, embracing him in a passionate kiss, as he reached a hand inside her shirt, popping the top two snaps of her bra open.

"Come on, Marissa," he teased. "Come with me."

She paused, then said, "I guess it wouldn't be so bad if I was fifteen or twenty minutes late," she said.

"Thirty."

"Done."

He smiled, trailing a finger up to her face. "Clock's ticking. Buckle up."

34

At twenty minutes past five, Quinn sat in a chair in the center of a semicircle with five out of eight of Evie's employees. Though they showed some interest in finding out what was going on, they looked tired, the vast majority slouching on chairs, eyeing Quinn like she didn't belong. The men in the group looked similar—all rough, outdoorsy types. Hard working. The skin on their hands was cracked and calloused, and they all wore ball caps except one, whose long, sandy-colored dreads were pulled back into a loose ponytail.

The two women were complete opposites from each other. The first appeared nervous and shy. She looked to be in her mid-twenties, and she wore a patterned pencil skirt and a white button-up. The second woman wore no makeup, and she looked just as tough as the guys, if not tougher.

After waiting a while for the last three employees to show up, Quinn decided she'd given the no-shows more than enough time to arrive.

"Thank you all for agreeing to meet with me tonight," Quinn said. "I believe you've all heard the rumors about me inheriting Evie's business. It's true. I just found out yesterday. I wanted to meet with you all tonight to give us all a chance to get to know each other."

The room went silent, no one wanting to be the first to speak up.

Quinn cleared her throat and continued. "Can each of you tell me your name and the position you have in Evie's company?"

Again, she was met with silence.

Quinn pointed to the woman in the pencil skirt. "Why don't we start with you and then go around?"

The woman batted her eyelashes and said, "I'm Felicity, the office manager. And I'm ... I mean I *was* Evie's assistant."

"It's nice to meet you, Felicity," Quinn said. "Evie was fond of you."

The office door blew open, and a man walked in.

He nodded at everyone and then took a seat, saying, "Why's everyone so quiet?"

"I've just asked everyone to tell me their name and what role they have here. So far, Felicity's been the only one to speak up."

"I'll go. Name's Rowdy. These other misfits are Axel, Ian, Carl, and Lin. Felicity works in the office, as she might have told you. The rest of us, the ones who are here, spend our days outside doing the dirty work."

As the ringleader of the group, Quinn's challenge was obvious—win Rowdy over and win over the rest. Pleasantries out of the way, the meeting entered phase two with rapid-fire questions from the group, including:

Was Quinn going to close the business?

Or sell it?

Were their jobs secure?

What did she know about landscaping?

Why had Evie left the business to her?

Quinn's efforts to squash their concerns with the truth fell flat, and she soon felt overwhelmed.

Not only did they not trust her, they didn't believe her either.

Just as the meeting seemed to be at a standstill, Ruby waltzed inside, Jacob in tow. Ruby sent him to play in an indoor playhouse in the corner, a wooden floor-to-ceiling structure Evie had constructed just for him.

"Ruby, what are you doing here?" Quinn asked. "I thought you were dropping Jacob off later this evening. Where is he?"

"He's in the car with your mother. She stopped by my house, and we decided the three of us would go to dinner. I heard you called a meeting, and thought I'd join in. *If* you don't mind having me here."

"You *heard* I was having a meeting?"

Ruby tipped her head. "Felicity called me."

"Why?"

"I know how feisty this lot can be. I don't mean to be an interruption. Carry on."

Carry on?

With Ruby listening in, Quinn was at a loss for what to say next.

She felt distracted, questioning Ruby's true intentions for being there.

"I ... umm ... I was just answering some questions everyone had about the future of the business," Quinn said.

"And how would you say it's going?"

"It's ... you know ... it's going."

"Mind if I have a short word with everyone?"

Although concerned about what "short words" Ruby had in mind, Quinn was out of ideas. "I guess so."

Ruby removed her jacket, placing it on the table as she

walked to the center of the circle. "You're all sitting here like a group of children who just dropped your lollipops in the sand. Whether your sad faces are over the loss of my precious grand-daughter or the future of your job, and I imagine it's a bit of both. Evie's business doesn't deserve to suffer just because someone new has entered the picture."

"What would you have us do?" Rowdy grunted.

"I know you all have your doubts. Some of you have called me. Others have been running around town this afternoon, gossiping about Quinn after you learned she's taking over the business. You haven't even given her a chance yet. If you cared for Evie, and if you care to see her business succeed for years to come, the gossip stops now."

"What does Quinn know about running a landscaping busi-ness, much less a business at all?" Rowdy asked.

"Quinn may not be up to speed on how Evie ran things yet, but she knows how much this place meant to her," Ruby said. "I know her well enough to say she'll give everything she has to keep it going."

"Ruby's right," Quinn said. "I will."

"You heard the woman," Ruby said. "And to keep things going, she'll need all of you. You've been here, you've worked here, side by side with Evie, most of you for several years. Right now, you're afraid. Even you men. Don't bother denying it either. And listen, I don't fault you for your feelings. We all have them, and tension's running high of late. Embrace your fears and then toss them aside. It does you no good to harbor ill will toward a person who's just trying to help."

"What you're asking ... it's a lot," Rowdy said. "With Evie gone, we're still trying to get our bearings."

"The first thing you all need to do is to get off your derrieres and get back to work. You know who your clients are, and you know the routine. It's business as usual. Burying my granddaughter was hard enough. I'm not going to sit around and watch her business get buried along with her."

"And if we can't get things back on track?" Rowdy asked. "Then what?"

"If any of you don't have the backbone to stick around, I would encourage you to bow out now. Get up and get out. If you stay, you agree to give Quinn a fair shot. You agree to help her with anything she needs. Have I made myself clear?"

No one spoke, at first.

"I'm in!" Felicity said.

"Good."

Ruby racked up verbal agreements from everyone in attendance, all except for one.

"Cat got your tongue, Rowdy?" Ruby asked.

"I … ahh … I don't know, Ruby. You needing an answer right now doesn't give me time to think."

"I'll need a commitment from you, Rowdy. Everyone else in attendance here tonight has made one. You don't get a free pass just because you managed the crew."

"Like I said, I need time."

"Then I believe you're done for tonight. You can go."

Rowdy stood, glaring at Ruby as he headed for the door.

"Wait, Rowdy," Quinn said. "Can we talk outside for a minute?"

He turned back, glaring at her. "No."

The door slammed behind him, and Ruby turned to Quinn. "Don't worry; he'll be back. If not tonight, tomorrow, I expect. Is there anything you'd like to add?"

Quinn looked at Felicity. "Aside from Marissa, who else didn't show up for the meeting?"

"Gage."

"And what does he do?" Quinn asked.

"Same as us," Lin said.

"If both of them care about the business, they should have been here." Ruby pulled Quinn to the side. "You're the boss now. The decisions you make from here on out will solidify you as one of two things—either as a person your employees respect or a person they feel like they can walk all over."

Quinn cleared her throat.

She wanted to be firm, yet diplomatic in her approach.

"Felicity, get me Marissa and Gage's phone numbers, please," she said. "I'll give them both a call tonight, see why they couldn't make the meeting."

Ruby smiled as if pleased. "I believe my job is done here. You're going to do a great job, Quinn, I just know it. I hope you don't mind me barging in. Rest assured; I won't get involved in the future. Unless you need me, of course."

35

After Ruby made her exit, Quinn hoped those in attendance would be open to the meeting going on a bit longer, but as she looked around, it became clear everyone was getting restless.

"I need to get home to my family," Lin said. "Can we call it a night and talk more later?"

"If you can stay for a few more minutes, I have some questions I wanted to ask."

"We've been here for over an hour already. This work stuff will have to wait until tomorrow. I got kids."

"I promise to be brief."

Lin placed a hand on her hip. "What is it, then?"

"Did any of you know Ray?"

"He came around here and there," Lin said.

"What do you think of him?"

"Ray's a sorry sap, but if you're thinking he killed Evie, my money wouldn't be on him."

"Why not?"

"Gut feeling. He puts on a tough front, but I think a lot of it is for show."

Quinn glanced around. "What do the rest of you think?"

"I don't know," Axel said. "I never knew the guy. We weren't a big part of her personal life."

"I agree," Ian added. "We haven't had the chance to get to know him."

Carl nodded.

Quinn got the distinct feeling there was more they wanted to say but didn't. She guessed it was because they didn't know her well enough to trust her with their true feelings.

One step forward, two steps back.

It was the way things had gone all day.

"I have to go," Lin said. "I told my husband I wouldn't be too late. He's not keen on tending the kids at night without me."

"I understand. Thank you all for taking the time to meet with me tonight."

One by one, everyone filed out, all except for Felicity, who smiled at Quinn and said, "You look worried."

"I am. I don't even know if they'll show up for work tomorrow."

"They'll stick around. Everyone who works here wants to keep Evie's business running as much as you do. Well, everyone except Gage. I know I can't speak for him, but even though he hasn't been here as long as the others, he's a hard worker. I thought he would have been here."

"What's his story?"

"Evie hired Gage to help Rowdy, and from day one, they butted heads."

"Having met Rowdy, I can see why."

"Rowdy put on a tough act for you tonight, but the truth is, he's a likable guy with a great sense of humor once he feels like he can trust you. You'll see. I think he's hard on Gage because he sees a little of himself in Gage. Maybe Rowdy thinks being tough on him will help him somehow."

"What makes you say that?"

"Something I overheard Rowdy say to Evie recently."

It was the most helpful advice Quinn had received all night.

"I'll talk to Gage," Quinn said.

"And Marissa?"

"When we met earlier today, I was sure she'd be at the meeting. I'm surprised she wasn't. Any idea why she missed it?"

"Not a clue. I had a work question before the meeting, and I called her. She said she'd just left her house, and she was heading this way."

"That's strange."

"She's reliable most of the time. But I've seen her change plans on a dime if something better comes up."

"I bet she wouldn't have missed a meeting with Evie," Quinn said.

"No, she wouldn't."

"If she was walking, she must not live far from here."

"About a mile or so."

It didn't make sense.

Even if Marissa had changed her mind, why would she do it when she was already on her way?

"Can you get me Marissa's address and phone number?" Quinn asked.

Felicity nodded and left the room.

The office door opened, and a man walked in. He was tall, slender, and looked to be in his late twenties, with a trimmed goatee and bangs that fell to his ears on both sides. He looked refined in a pair of fitted slacks and a crisp, navy button-up shirt.

Thinking he was a client, Quinn said, "We're closed."

"I know," he said. "I'm Gabe. Sorry I'm late. I got a flat tire."

"Was your cell phone dead too, because you could have called."

"I ... yeah, you're right. Sorry."

"I don't need you to be sorry. I need you to communicate."

"I called Rowdy. He didn't answer."

"I hear the two of you don't get along," Quinn said.

"We don't agree on everything, but we make it work."

Quinn sighed. "Well, you've missed the meeting."

"I'm here now."

"I'm too tired to fill you in on what we talked about tonight."

"I still have my job, though, right?"

Quinn tapped her boot to the floor, thinking. "Tell me why I should keep you."

Felicity walked back into to the room, blushing when she saw Gage.

"Oh, Gage, hi," Felicity said. "I'm glad you made it or tried to make it or whatever. I mean, you're here now, which is good."

Her eyes darted to the floor, and she ran a finger over some locks of her hair, tucking it behind her ear.

Felicity liked Gage, that much was obvious.

"Gage, I'm about to head out," Quinn said. "Let's talk later."

"When's a good time?"

"I'll give you a call tomorrow or the next day."

"Should I show up for work?"

"I suppose that will be fine."

"Thanks, ahh ..."

"Quinn."

"Good to meet you."

She thought about saying the same but didn't.

She also didn't say anything to Felicity about her obvious crush.

Felicity cleared her throat and handed Quinn a green folder.

"I've made you a list with every employee's address and phone number. I also made a list earlier today with all the appointments we've had so far this year and every job we have for the rest of the year."

"I appreciate everything you've done to help me, Felicity. If you hear from Marissa, please let me know."

36

Janae Burgess sat at a charming bistro table, its top made up of tiny square tiles in the shape of a large sunflower.

She took a sip of her Italian soda and frowned. The drink had almost no carbonation and lacked in flavor, tasting more like bland vanilla than the tart burst she'd expected. At almost seven dollars, she felt ripped off. She considered going up to the counter to see if they'd make her a new one, but she didn't. She was not a fan of confrontation and avoided it whenever possible.

Across the street was Evie's landscaping business. As Janae watched out the window, she saw a young woman hand Quinn a folder and then something else, something too small to identify—a key maybe. The woman waved goodbye and left, leaving Quinn in the shop alone.

Janae had been tossing around the idea of finding a way to speak to Quinn alone. Seeing her now, it almost seemed like fate, like the decision had been made for her. She stood, tossed the soda in the trash can, looking both ways before jaywalking across the street.

She arrived in time to see Quinn locking the shop door.

Quinn turned and hopped back, pressing a hand to her chest.

"Sorry, I didn't mean to sneak up on you," Janae said. "I need to talk to you."

"Sure, what's going on?"

Janae's eyes danced around, surveying the street, the sidewalk. There were a few people milling around, and given Cody was a small town, the thought of someone overhearing their conversation made her uncomfortable.

"I know you just locked up, but would it be all right if we talked inside?" she asked.

Quinn nodded, reopened the office door, and both ladies stepped inside.

"All right," Quinn said. "What did you want to talk to me about?"

"What you're thinking, or what I assume you're thinking about Ray ... well, you're wrong. He didn't kill Evie."

"How can you be so sure?"

Janae looked down, eyes focused on the gooseflesh trailing up and down her own arms. It wasn't because she was cold. She felt queasy, like everything in her body was out of sync.

"Whatever it is, you can tell me," Quinn said.

"I ... I was there."

"You were *where*?"

"At Evie's house the night she died."

"Have you told the police?"

"Umm, no. You're the first person I've told. Thing is, I wasn't alone. I was with Ray."

Quinn crossed her arms, her expression one of confusion and disappointment, making Janae feel even worse than she already did.

"Why haven't you said anything to anyone until now?"

"Let me explain. Ray wasn't his usual self that day. He was

struggling over the breakup. I felt bad for him, and when we finished work for the day, I asked if he wanted to talk. He suggested we go for a drive, and we did."

"What happened during the drive?"

"After I got into the truck, Ray said he needed to stop by Evie's place to get his fishing equipment. I didn't like the idea. I didn't want her to see us together. He pacified me by suggesting I stay in the car. It was dark out, and on the off chance she saw me, he was going to say we were together for a work-related thing."

"What time did this happen?"

"The same time he told you earlier today."

"How long was the visit?"

"Five minutes tops. Ray said a quick hello to Evie and to Jacob, he grabbed his stuff, and we left."

"Five minutes is long enough to kill someone."

"It's not possible."

"Why not?" Quinn asked.

"Evie was in the doorway when he left. I saw her say goodbye to him."

"Did Ray drop you back off at your vehicle? If he did, he could have driven back to Evie's house and murdered her then. Maybe what happened with you was planned. He knew you were vulnerable and figured you'd make a good alibi."

"I get why you think that, but no."

"What do you mean *no*?"

Janae took in a deep breath, not wanting to say what was coming next, but knowing for Ray's sake, she had to say it. "Ray *didn't* drop me off after we left Evie's house."

"What do you mean?"

"I didn't go home until the next morning."

"Why not?"

"My husband was working the night shift, and our kids

were staying at my parents' house. I went to Ray's place, and, you know, all we did was talk at first, but then we ... umm ..."

"Are you saying the two of you slept together?"

Struggling to keep eye contact, Janae bowed her head. "It was an accident. I love my husband. It's not Ray's fault. I made a choice. The wrong choice. I let my emotions get the best of me. It was only supposed to be a one-time thing."

"When I saw you at Ray's house, I'm guessing it happened again?"

A tear ran down Janae's cheek, and she grabbed Quinn's arm. "Please, Quinn. Things haven't been the best with my husband in the last few months, and look, I know it's not a good enough excuse for what I did. I screwed up, and the guilt I feel is overwhelming. If my husband finds out, it's over between us."

"I'm not going to say anything to your husband," Quinn said.

In recent months, Janae been starved for attention, married to a man who no longer looked at her the way he once did. All she wanted was to feel attractive again, to feel wanted and seen. Ray had filled that void. And yet, she was riddled with guilt.

"I thought you said sleeping with Ray was an accident?" Quinn asked.

"I suppose I convinced myself we'd already done the deed once, so what difference would a few more times make? Besides, everyone in town thinks Roman killed Evie, so I didn't see why I needed to confess what happened that night."

"It doesn't matter what people think. You kept an important piece of information from the police. I get why you did it, but it's still wrong."

Janae walked to the front desk, grabbed a tissue out of the box, and blotted her eyes. "I'm sorry I didn't say something before."

"Why risk everything now?" Quinn asked. "And why tell me, of all people?"

"When you accused Ray today, I knew I had to do something. I can't let him get charged for a crime he didn't commit, even if it means the truth comes out and I lose my marriage over it."

"You realize confessing to the police now will make you look like a suspect too, right? You slept with a man who's a murder suspect. They might not believe your story. They might think you're coming forward as his alibi, so he doesn't get charged for Evie's murder."

"Neither of us had anything to do with Evie's murder. Everything I told you just now is the truth. I swear."

Quinn leaned against the wall, crossing one leg over the other, trying to decide whether she believed her.

"If Ray didn't kill Evie, the question remains—who did?" Quinn asked.

Janae raised a finger. "I may be able to help with that. After we left Evie's house we were driving down the road, and I saw a truck sitting off to the side. It wasn't running. It was turned off, like it had been parked there. I didn't think anything of it before now, and because it was so dark, I couldn't tell if anyone was inside."

"Where on the road was the truck parked?"

"Not far from Mrs. Healy's house."

37

Sitting at a table at an upscale restaurant with Simone, Bo found it hard to believe it had only been a week since they last saw each other. So much had transpired in the time she'd been away—those seven days felt like a lifetime.

When they first met, Bo thought Simone might be the kind of girl he could have a future with one day. She was easy on the eyes, bright, and funny, and things between them had been going well.

So why was he feeling so unsettled?

As he glanced at her across the table, he felt like he was picking her apart, focusing on her flaws and imperfections. Since they'd been seated, she'd cracked her knuckles at least a dozen times.

Had she always done that?

If so, why hadn't he noticed before?

Or had he, except it hadn't bugged him before, and now it did.

Every woman he'd dated since Quinn were mostly short-term relationships. If he was being honest with himself, the women were all wonderful in their own ways, but there was one thing they were not—*her*.

"Did you miss me?" Simone asked. "I missed you."

"I've been looking forward to seeing you," he said. "So much has happened since you've been away."

"What did you do while I was gone?"

"I've been working, a lot more than usual."

"Oh, yeah, on the murder investigation. How's it going? Are you getting anywhere?"

"Not as far as I would like."

"You haven't looked at your cell phone once since we got to the restaurant," she said. "I appreciate it. I'm sure it's hard not to keep checking it with all that's going on right now."

She was right.

He wasn't checking his phone.

But it wasn't for the reason she assumed.

In his haste to meet her at the restaurant on time, he'd dropped it, the front cracking as it hit the ground. He hoped it wasn't broken, but when he picked it up, it wouldn't turn back on. And given his cellular provider was already closed, he'd have to wait until tomorrow to replace it.

"Bo?" she asked.

"Yeah?"

"You seem ... I don't know, distant tonight. You haven't said much since we sat down. It's like you're here, but you're not here, if that makes sense."

"It does, and I'm sorry. I have a lot on my mind right now."

She reached across the table, turning his face toward her. "Talk to me. Tell me what's going on."

What *was* going on? He wasn't even sure.

His head was all over the place, filled with uncertainty.

"Something's different," she pressed. "Did something else happen while I was away?"

"Evie and I have been friends since we were kids. It's one of the reasons I'm so focused on this case."

Simone dipped a piece of bread into her soup, nodding. "It makes sense. I'm sure it's hard to talk about. Why don't we start with you telling me about your day?"

Bo set his fork down and looked around. Given how busy the restaurant was, he doubted anyone would overhear their conversation. Still, he was leery about discussing the investigation in public.

Lowering his voice, he said, "I questioned Ray Ferguson again, Evie's ex-boyfriend. Got a different story this time around."

"Is he your main suspect?"

"He's one of them. Quinn got in his face a bit, but it wasn't enough to convince me of his guilt."

Simone grabbed her napkin, clenching it in her hand. "Did you just say *Quinn*—as in the woman you dated in high school?"

He hadn't meant to mention Quinn.

Her name just slipped out.

Too late to take it back now.

"I did," he said. "I was planning on talking to you about her tonight once we—"

Simone raised a hand. "Hold on. I thought you said you hadn't seen or talked to in ages."

"I haven't. It's complicated."

"And today, are you saying you were *with* her? The two of you were together while I was away?"

"Here and there. Quinn and Evie were best friends."

"She doesn't live here, though, and Evie's funeral was several days ago. What's she still doing in Cody?"

Simone's tone had changed, becoming accusatory and short.

"Like I said before, a lot has happened while you were way," he said.

She crossed her arms, leaning back in the chair. "For example?"

"Evie left her business to Quinn, and she left guardianship of her son to Quinn as well. Quinn's staying with her family while she figures things out."

"And just how long will it take for her to *figure things out*, Bo?"

She'd raised her voice, causing several of the restaurant's patrons to look their way.

"Let's not talk about this here," Bo said. "We should have this conversation in private."

"Who cares if people are listening?"

"Please, Simone. Let's finish our meal. Then we can go to my place and talk."

Simone leaned back, narrowing her eyes. "You're acting weird, and I don't think the murder investigation is the only reason. You've always had a thing for Quinn, and here I was thinking she was out of your life for good. If we're going to keep dating, you need to promise me you won't ever see her again."

"And if I do see her?"

"We're over. What's it going to be?"

Bo had never been fond of threats and ultimatums. The pushback from Simone was a side of her he hadn't seen, one she'd kept hidden until now. On one hand, he understood. She felt threatened by Quinn's return to town, and she had a right to feel the way she was feeling. On the other, they'd only been on a handful of dates. Sure, he wasn't seeing anyone else, but the way he saw it, they weren't even in an official relationship yet.

"I can't continue this conversation," he said. "Not here."

"It's unacceptable, Bo. I'm not interested in talking later. I want to finish this conversation, here and now."

Seeing no positive way out, he tossed his napkin on the table and stood. "You can stay if you like, or you can follow me home and we can talk there. Either way, I'm going to pay the check, and then I'm leaving."

38

With the landscape meeting still weighing on Quinn's mind, there were a couple stops she wanted to make before returning home. She called to check in on Jacob, and her mother said he was in good spirits, but tired and ready for bed. He would spend the night there, which pleased Quinn.

They ended the call, and she drove down the long, windy dirt road, her thoughts shifting to Bo. She wondered how things were going with Simone. Each time he'd entered her thoughts that day, she'd tried to push them down. But no matter how hard she tried, the thoughts kept coming, a fact she couldn't ignore.

She pulled her father's car to a stop in front of a quaint country farmhouse, walked to the front door, and knocked. A husky, redheaded woman dressed in men's sweatpants and a hoodie opened the door and smiled, saying, "Can I help you?"

"I was wondering if Marissa is at home?"

The woman shook her head. "She's gone into town for a work meeting, though I thought it would be over by now."

"It is over. The meeting was with me."

"Oh, you must be Evie's friend, Quinn, right? I'm Yvonne. It's wonderful to meet you."

"And you. I'm here because Marissa never showed up for the meeting."

The woman's face went blank. "I don't understand. I had a chat with her right before she left, and she told me she was about to head to town for the meeting."

"I haven't seen your daughter since we met earlier today. Does she have a boyfriend or a friend she may have decided to hang out with instead?"

"Marissa has a lot of boys who are friends, but friends are all they are. She doesn't have time for a boyfriend."

"Why not?"

"She'll be off to college soon. She plans to be a pediatric doctor."

A doctor?

Marissa had said she wanted to be a landscape artist.

It seemed mother and daughter were not on the same page.

Yvonne reached into her pants pocket, pulling out her cell phone. "Let me give Marissa a call, see where she's at."

She made the call, her expression souring as she said, "How odd. It went straight to voicemail."

"Does she usually answer your calls?"

"Most of the time, yes."

A man approached from behind, his hand coming to rest on Yvonne's shoulder. "Honey, what's this about Marissa?"

Yvonne turned toward him. "I'm not sure, Ron. This is Quinn. She's the woman Marissa was telling us about, the one who's taking over Evie's business."

Ron gave me a nod, saying, "Good to meet you."

"I was hoping Marissa was here," Quinn said. "She never showed up for the work meeting."

"Huh, I'll bet she's out running around. She's a teenager.

Teenagers don't always do what they're supposed to do when they're supposed to do it. You remember what it was like at that age, don't you?"

Quinn did.

Still ... something didn't feel right.

"When she left your house earlier today, she told your wife she was going to the meeting. Then one of the other women working in the office also spoke to her, and Marissa said the same thing," I said. "Now she's not answering her cell phone. Doesn't that seem strange to you?"

"I must say, the more we talk about it, the more uneasy I feel," Yvonne said. "Marissa is a responsible young woman. Teenager or not, she's a good girl. She doesn't get into mischief."

Ron's eyes widened, his expression conveying he disagreed with Yvonne's opinion, but he remained silent.

"If you see Marissa, will you ask her to call me?" Quinn asked.

"You bet," Yvonne said. "Let me take down your number."

Yvonne disappeared into the kitchen, returning with a notepad and pen. Quinn scribbled her number down and then handed it back, adding, "Please let her know I need to speak with her—sooner than later."

39

Quinn reached for her phone, trying to decide who to call first. She knew who she *wanted* to call, but she couldn't bring herself to do it. Instead, she sent Bo a quick text message and then called Kyle.

When he answered, she blurted out, "I have a problem. Well, what I'm trying to say is, I'm worried about one of Evie's employees. Her name is Marissa Lewis. I saw her this morning, and I decided to set up a meeting with the crew to introduce myself and ask questions about the transition now that Evie's gone. Marissa said she'd be there, but she didn't show. I went to her house, and she's not there either. Her mother tried to call her, and she didn't answer. I've sent Bo a text message, but he hasn't responded."

Not that she expected he would.

With Simone back in town, his girlfriend would be his priority.

"You mean you have *two* problems, right?" Kyle said.

His tone was somber, unlike his usual upbeat self.

"Uhh ... no, just the one problem," she said.

"I see you took it upon yourself to keep Ray from leaving town."

"I don't know what you're talking about."

"It's me you're talking to, Quinn, and it's all right. Your secret's safe with me, so you can tell the truth. You're not going to get in trouble."

The truth about what?

"I spoke with Ray earlier today," she said. "We exchanged a few words. I haven't seen him since."

"Wanna guess where I am right now?"

"I'd rather you just tell me."

"I'm at Ray's house, standing on his front lawn, admiring your handiwork."

"What *handiwork*?"

"You can cut the innocent act, Quinn. Ray knows you did it."

"Did what?"

"All of his tires are flat. They've been slashed."

Quinn thought back to her conversation with Ruby.

Perhaps *she* had slashed his tires.

"I didn't do it, Kyle. I swear. How could I? I was in a meeting with Evie's employees this evening. A half a dozen people can vouch for me."

"Look, I get it. I'd like nothing more than to prove he's responsible for Evie's murder, but there's a chance he isn't."

Had Janae already been to the police?

Had the truth about that night come out—*if*, in fact it was the truth?

"Why do you think Ray might be innocent?" Quinn asked.

"Shouldn't be telling you this, but a witness came forward tonight. Ray has an alibi, and not just for the time surrounding the murder, but for the entire night."

"I know about your witness," she said. "Janae stopped by

the office tonight after the meeting. I'm guessing she told you the same thing she told me."

"I'm guessing you're right."

"How do you know she's telling the truth?" Quinn asked.

"I don't. Felt like there were inconsistencies between her story and his, and he's lied before, so it's hard to know what to believe. Just when we think we're getting somewhere with this case, everything shifts. It's frustrating. Anyway, back to Marissa, what would you like me to do?"

"I was hoping you or Bo could keep an eye out."

"How long has she been missing?"

"A few hours."

"Hmm … well, not enough time has passed to us to put a BOLO out yet, but yeah, I'll keep my eyes peeled."

"I appreciate it."

"Hey … ahh, I have to say, I'm surprised you called, but I'm glad you did."

"Why are you surprised?" Quinn asked.

"I thought we had a good time hanging out the other night. Did I say or do something to offend you?"

"Of course, not."

"Well, something must have happened. And hey, I understand. If you want me to back off, I will."

"I don't know what you mean. I haven't asked you to back off."

Kyle sighed, then said, "I was talking to Bo earlier today, and I told him I had plans to ask you out again. He made it clear you had no interest in me other than being friends. Hey, I'm glad he told me, but next time, I'd appreciate it if you told me yourself."

40

Bo telling Kyle she wasn't interested left Quinn with mixed feelings. While she didn't appreciate what he'd done, she wondered why he'd done it. He was in a relationship with someone else. He had no right to stop her from seeing Kyle if she wanted to, something she'd be sure to tell him when she saw him again.

For now, she set aside her thoughts and stepped up to Rowdy's front porch.

He opened the door, head shaking as he said, "What do *you* want?"

Beer bottle in hand, he barely made eye contact with Quinn before turning around and returning to his old, ratty recliner. She remained where she was for a moment, unsure if the open door was an invitation to come in or whether it wasn't.

Hand palming the gun inside her purse, she said, "Can I talk to you? I won't take long."

"The game's on. I'm busy."

Quinn took a chance and stepped inside. "Who's playing?"

Eyes glued to the television, he said, "You expect me to believe *you* follow football?"

"When I'm with my dad. He's a Raiders fan, which makes me one too. What about you?"

"Well, what do you know. Sounds like we have one shared interest."

Quinn had hoped a little sports banter might lighten things up between them, until he clicked a button on the television remote, increasing the volume.

She cupped a hand to the side of her mouth and raised her voice. "I just need five minutes of your time."

He took another swig of beer, made a two-pointer into a plastic wastebasket several feet away, and stood, scratching his chest as he walked to the kitchen. "Like I said, I'm watching the game."

"Can you pause it for a second?"

He cracked open a fresh can of beer and said, "Two minutes."

"Five. And if you want to keep negotiating, I can leave, and you'll lose the chance to keep your job."

"What makes you think I want it?"

"You want it more than anyone who works there. You were frustrated earlier today, which is understandable. You're passionate about your job—you care about it. I can tell. It's not just a job. You take pride in what you do."

He cocked a brow. "You got all that from one meeting?"

"You were Evie's go-to person, the one who managed everything. Right?"

He belched and turned toward Quinn. "Wanna beer?"

"No, thanks."

He laughed. "Worried it will ruin your girlish figure?"

"I appreciate the offer. I just don't care much for beer."

"Suit yourself."

He returned to the recliner, grabbed the remote, and sat a minute, thinking.

Then he paused the television and looked over at her. "Five minutes. Ticktock."

"How old are you?" Quinn asked.

"You came all the way here tonight to ask me about my age? I'm twenty-three. And you?"

"Add a few years and you're there," she said. "You were young when you started working for Evie."

"Still in high school. She helped me through a difficult time in my life."

"Yeah, I know. Had to do with drugs, didn't it?"

He went silent, studying her for a moment.

At last.

She had his full attention.

"How do you know about my past?" he asked.

"Evie told me."

"At the meeting today, you acted like you didn't know a thing about me. You acted like you didn't know a thing about any of us."

"Evie didn't talk about many of her employees, but she mentioned you from time to time. She said you were the one person she could count on no matter what. That's why she put you in charge last year. To be honest, having you to lean on kept her sane during her divorce. With you there, she felt she could take a break from work without worrying about her clients suffering in her absence. The way you stepped up, it meant a lot to her."

"I would have done anything for that woman. She was a good friend. The best person I've ever known."

"I know," Quinn said. "So, please, stay. Work with me. I need you. I'm not trying to take over. I'm just trying to keep it going. With Marissa not showing up, we're already down one person. I don't want to make it two."

He turned toward Quinn, looking confused. "Are you saying Marissa never showed after I left?"

"She didn't."

He went quiet, giving Quinn the feeling there was something he wasn't saying.

"Is there anything I should know?" she asked.

"I was gonna call her after the game to ask her what happened during the meeting after I left. That's all."

Only it *wasn't* all.

Quinn could tell.

He'd wiped his brow twice in the past minute alone.

"You want to know something," Quinn said. "I thought Ray killed Evie. After the meeting with the crew, I found out Ray might have a solid alibi during the time Evie was murdered."

"How do you know the alibi is reliable?"

"I don't. Guess we'll have to wait and see. You knew Evie well. Who do you think did it?"

He gave the question some thought. "I knew every person in her life. At least, I think I did. Not a single one of them seem capable of murder."

"What if it wasn't a friend or a lover? What if it was a client?"

Rowdy raised a brow. "It's a gardening business. You get that, right? We're fair, honest, and on time, every time. We meet all our deadlines. No one has ever made a complaint that Evie didn't make right."

Another dead end.

It was worth a try.

"Well, I promised five minutes, and my time is just about up, so I'll go, leave you to finish your game in peace," Quinn said. "See you at work tomorrow?"

"What about what Ruby said earlier?"

Quinn swished a hand through the air and winked. "What about it? *I'm* in charge now."

41

A faint breeze blew rhythm into a wind chime dangling from a string between two wooden slats on Rowdy's porch. And then there was a crack, a faint rustling sound vibrating from the edge of the property, between the trees. Quinn squinted, staring at them like she expected someone to jump out from between them, but no one did, at first. Then she looked up, spotting an owl peering down at her. She breathed a sigh of relief, picking up the pace as she made her way to the car.

Questions filled her mind.

If Ray didn't murder Evie, who did?

Rowdy was someone Evie had trusted.

But what if there was another side to him, a side no one could see.

Perhaps he'd had a motive to murder Evie, one that hadn't presented itself yet.

And where was Marissa?

Quinn hoped the girl had made it home by now.

From the safe confines of the vehicle, Quinn locked the doors, flipping the high beams on as she pulled out of Rowdy's driveway. Even with the headlights on, the night was shrouded in fog, and she squinted to distinguish the lanes in the road. She gripped the steering wheel tight, doing her best to focus.

The roads she often traveled around town were, of course, familiar, and easy to navigate. But the one leading away from Rowdy's place left her feeling like she was going in circles. After some time, it became evident she'd been driving along the same streets, her sense of direction falling as the minutes passed. And then, there it was, the familiar road, leading back to town.

Quinn turned onto the main road, exhaling what felt like the first real breath she'd taken in some time. She'd driven less than a quarter of a mile when she noticed a vehicle approaching from behind. It was coming up fast, its headlights blinding as they reflected back at her in the rear window.

Hoping she could get the vehicle to pass by, she jerked the steering wheel to the right, giving the other driver the road. She assumed the gesture would work ... until it didn't. The vehicle sped up, ramming into her back bumper before swerving around the driver's side of the car. Then it darted up the up the road and out of sight.

As the car spiraled out of control, Quinn braced the wheel for support.

For a moment, she did nothing, the shock of the crash causing her to relive her previous accident all over again. Coming to her senses, she tapped on the brake, and the car jolted to a stop. As she sat in silence, catching her breath, she began to process what had just happened.

She looked around.

The truck was gone.

The street was empty.

The nightmare she'd just endured seemed to be over.

But was it?

It wasn't hard to figure out who'd hit her and why.

Someone wanted to send her a message.

Someone who knew she was going around town, asking questions.

Too many questions.

The soft blur of headlights slowed to a stop behind her. Her first instinct was to panic, to assume the man who'd just rammed had returned, that he was coming for her a second time. As she reached for her gun, she looked in the rearview mirror, noticing the vehicle behind her wasn't a truck. It was a sedan.

An older woman approached Quinn's car, tapping on her window and saying, "Ma'am, are you all right?"

Quinn shook her head, allowing the tears she'd been holding back to fall.

"No," she said. "No, I'm not."

42

The woman who'd come to Quinn's aid called for an ambulance, and then she ran to her car, grabbing a blanket. She brought it back, handed it to Quinn, and said, "I'll stay with you until help arrives, okay? Everything going to be fine, sweetie."

Minutes passed, thought it felt like hours, and then the ambulance arrived. Quinn was escorted out of the car to the back of the van where a paramedic began to check her for injuries. It wasn't long before another vehicle rolled up, and Kyle stepped out, rushing to her side.

"I just heard," he said. "Are you okay?"

"Yeah, I have a few bruises, but no broken bones or anything."

"What happened?"

"I was on my way back to my parents' house, and I noticed a truck coming up behind me. It was going a lot faster than it should have been. Its brights were on, and the driver side-swiped me and then took off."

Kyle clicked his flashlight on, excusing himself for a moment to inspect the exterior of the car. Soon after, a squad car pulled up. Kyle walked over, and Quinn overheard him telling the two officers it was a hit-and-run. The three of them walked over to the car to inspect it, and Kyle said the truck involved may have been white or silver, as evidenced by the streaks of paint embedded in Quinn's car. Given it was dark out, it would be hard to know for certain until morning.

After the conversation ended, Kyle returned to Quinn, asking the paramedics if she was free to go. She was given the all-clear, and Kyle said, "Do you feel up to filling out a report?"

"Yeah, sure."

"All right, come with me."

He escorted Quinn to his vehicle. She got inside, and he handed her a clipboard along with a pen.

"Sit tight, and fill out what you can for me," he said. "We're going to need to tow the car."

"It's my dad's. I can't stop thinking about he's going to feel when he sees it all busted up."

"I'm certain your dad's concern will be for your safety, not for the car. What happened tonight wasn't your fault."

"I still feel bad."

"Listen, I'll be right back, and then I'll drive you home, okay?"

Quinn thanked him for the offer but let him know she'd already called someone else, the only person she knew to call. All she needed to do now was to sit and wait.

Once the form was as filled out, Kyle slid back into the driver's seat, a look of concern on his face as he turned toward her. "Listen, are you sure you're okay?"

"I'm not sure of anything."

"I know it's dark out, making it hard for you to see who did this to you, but do you mind telling me again what happened? As best as you can remember. Start from when you were hit and then tell me where you were tonight, after your work meeting."

Quinn closed her eyes, wondering why Bo still hadn't shown up yet.

If Kyle had been made aware of the accident, wouldn't Bo have been too?

Where was he?

She pushed the thought to the side. "I turned onto the main road to town, and I noticed someone coming up behind me. It didn't look like they were going to slow down, and at first, I thought maybe they were distracted and didn't see me. Now I ... I don't know."

"Were your headlights on?"

"They were."

"What happened after you saw the other vehicle?"

"I tried to get out of the way. I thought if I pulled to the side, they'd go around. He hit me anyway ... or she."

"Do you think you were hit on purpose?"

"Maybe, I don't know. I mean, they kept going. It felt like it was on purpose."

He ran a hand through his hair, breathing out a frustrated sigh. "Let's talk about what you did this evening. Where have you been, and who have you seen?"

"I spent the evening with Evie's employees, as I told you earlier. We had a meeting."

"Aside from Marissa not showing up, how did the meeting go?"

"Not bad for the first one," she said.

"No one seemed angry or upset?"

Almost all of them did, but she wasn't about to admit it.

"It's hard to say," Quinn said. "They're not thrilled about me taking over Evie's business, but I don't know them well enough to tell you how they felt when the meeting was over. I'd like to think I'd reassured them, and we'll figure out the rest one step at a time."

"Did anything happen during the meeting, anything that could have set one of them off?"

Quinn could think of one thing.

"Ruby showed up in the middle of it."

Kyle raised a brow. "Why?"

"She said she came in to offer me support. I'll admit, she was a bit harsh, but they seemed to respect her. Well, all except for Rowdy. He was upset, and he left before the meeting ended."

She hadn't wanted to mention it all all, but it had to be said.

"When you say upset, how upset are we talking?" he asked.

"It's hard to say. I don't know the guy well enough yet."

"Did he threaten you in any way?"

"No, nothing like that."

"What happened after the meeting?"

Quinn considered what to say next.

"Janae stopped by, and when I think back on it now, it was a little weird," Quinn said. "It felt like she was watching and waiting for our meeting to end so we could talk. As soon as I locked up the office, she just appeared out of nowhere. It didn't take long for me to realize her agenda—convincing me Ray is innocent."

"Yeah, I thought the same thing when I talked to her today."

"I'm just not sure whether I believe her story."

He paused, then said, "You see or talk to anyone else after your meeting?"

"Because Marissa didn't show up for the meeting, I went to her parents' house to ask if they'd seen her. They hadn't. Then I went to Rowdy's place to see if I could smooth things over. I thought our conversation went as well as it could have. I didn't stay long. After I left, that's when I had the run-in with the truck, and here we are."

He jotted down a few things on a notepad. "Anything else I should know?"

"I don't think so. Hey ... uhh, I want to thank you."

"For what?"

"Waiting with me until my ride came."

"Hey, anytime. I'm glad you're safe."

"When we spoke on the phone earlier, what Bo said to you ... I just wanted to make it clear—I didn't have a conversation about you with him."

Kyle placed a hand on Quinn's arm. "I believe you. I was just ... I didn't handle our conversation well. After all these years, Bo still has a thing for you, though, doesn't he?"

"All I know is, his girlfriend's back in town now, and even if he wasn't dating her, I'm preoccupied with a lot of other things."

Preoccupied.

The biggest understatement of the year.

Ever since Evie died, she felt like she was being jerked in all directions.

"When we hung out the other night, it wasn't just about trying to get you to answer my questions," Quinn said. "I had dinner with you because I consider you a friend."

"Friends, huh? That all?"

"It is, Kyle."

Well ... all right. I'll take what I can get."

"You're disappointed. I can tell."

"It's just ..."

"Just what?"

He turned, thumbing in the direction of the car that had just pulled up alongside them. "Looks like your ride's here."

43

"Thanks for coming to pick me up," Quinn said.

Astrid turned the radio down and turned, offering Quinn a slight smile. "It's the least I could do after all that's happened. I'm guessing I wasn't the first person you called, which is understandable."

"I ... yeah, you're right. I tried Dad. He didn't pick up."

"He went to bed about an hour ago. I bet he didn't hear the phone ring."

"And Mom?"

"She's in the casita with Jacob, watching a movie. I'm guessing she left her phone in the house. She's forgetful that way. When I got your call, I wasn't sure whether you'd want them to know what's going on yet, so I didn't say anything. Are you all right?"

"I'll be fine, which is more than I can say for Dad's car."

"Oh, no."

"Oh, yes."

Quinn filled Astrid in on the details.

When she finished, Astrid said, "I don't think someone hit you by accident, Quinn. You were run off the road on purpose."

"Why would anyone target me? I might be asking questions about Evie's death, but I'm getting nowhere. I have no idea who killed her or why."

"I think you *think* you have it wrong, but I'm guessing you know more than you realize. Be more careful from now on, okay? You shouldn't be driving in the dark alone, not when Quinn's killer might still be around."

It was surreal, receiving advice from her younger sister, a sister who had always been the reckless one.

"You think someone was trying to scare me?" Quinn asked.

"Or worse. Ever since your call, I've been thinking about it."

"And?"

Astrid bit her lip. "I hate to suggest anyone without any proof, but what about Marcus?"

"What about him?"

"What if Marcus killed Evie? He hated her."

"He didn't hate her."

"Yes, he did. Think about it, Quinn. After you lost your son, your marriage unraveled. What if he blamed Evie?"

"Even if I entertained the idea for a second, I don't see how it could have been him. We were just getting back from our vacation when she died. And yeah, you're right. When anything went wrong with us, he blamed Evie and the influence he thought she had over me. But to murder her? I don't see it."

Astrid raised a finger. "Your vacation could have been part of a plan to make him seem innocent. He could have hired someone to do the job for him."

"I don't believe he's capable of murder."

Or was he, and she was being naïve not to consider him?

"At your wedding reception, Marcus told me he despised Evie. He used that word too—*despised*. I told him he'd better find a way to accept her, because she'd always be part of your life. He laughed and said I should never say never."

"I'm sure his comment was harmless, a way to make himself seem superior. Can we change the subject, please?"

For a time, there was silence between them.

Quinn stared out the window at nothing.

Astrid bobbed her head to tune playing on the radio.

"I ... umm ... I haven't seen you around much the last couple days," Astrid said. "I didn't know whether you were going out of your way to avoid me, or if you decided never to speak to me again, or what. I'm still planning on leaving town. I just haven't finalized my plans yet."

"What happened between us, what you did, Astrid ... I ended up making the biggest mistake of my life."

"I ... I was jealous of you. Jealous of what you had with Bo. I was young and stupid. I feel awful about it now, about all of it."

"You had so many years to make things right, and you didn't."

"I was going to tell you, and then you got pregnant. I was afraid of what would happen when the truth came out and everyone realized what a jerk I'd been. I know nothing I can say will ever change the past. What's done is done. But just know, I've carried the regret around with me for a long time. I always hoped to make it right."

Quinn wanted to believe her, to begin anew.

But there was still so much pain.

"In the note you left me, when you said I should come clean and tell the truth," Quinn said. "I assume you're referring to my son, Isaiah."

"If you're going to make things right with Bo, he may as well know all of it. He probably thinks you married Marcus for love, and no matter what you told everyone, we both know you didn't."

"I don't see how it would make a difference now. Bo's moved on."

Astrid reached out, patting her sister on the shoulder. "This is Bo we're talking about, sis. I don't believe for a second that he's ever moved on from you."

44

Quinn rested a bottle of water on the table next to her and reclined back against one of the plush pillows on the sofa. Whether she was ready to admit it or not, she had to accept the possibility that the car crash may not have been accidental. It may have been deliberate, the act of someone trying to scare her or to warn her: *this is what will happen if you don't stop sticking your nose where it doesn't belong.* If true, Evie's killer was nearby and perhaps assumed Quinn was a lot closer to discovering the truth.

With Ray's possible innocence, Quinn shifted her thinking.

Revenge.

Money.

Jealousy.

Secrets.

Each a driving force for murder.

One avenue she hadn't gone down was whether Evie's death may have been tied to her landscaping business somehow. Evie's appointment book was confusing and disorganized, much like Evie's personality in life. Almost everything in the job book was scribbled at an angle in blue pen and then highlighted with a neon marker.

There were two sides to Evie's business. The repeat side included yard maintenance, fertilizer, weed control, and in the winter months, snow removal. Almost all the work generated from that side of the business was overseen by Rowdy, who then delegated the jobs out to his crew.

The other side, landscaping, was overseen by Evie and included existing contracts with two builders in town and jobs requested by the homeowners themselves. Of the two builders, one was just breaking ground on a new subdivision, and the other had just finished, which meant Evie hadn't been working with either of them before her death.

Quinn spread all the recent work invoices on the coffee table in front of her. She picked out the ones Rowdy was responsible for, deciding, with Rowdy at the helm, Evie wouldn't have been as involved. Next she removed the ones that had gone out to the builders whose jobs hadn't started yet. This left three current landscaping jobs, all of them for local homeowners.

She clicked on her cell phone and checked the time. It was after midnight. Too late to give Felicity a ring. For now, her questions would have to wait.

Quinn raised both hands over her head and yawned. The melatonin she'd found in the kitchen cabinet appeared to be kicking in. She stood and started to draw the kitchen curtains closed, stopping when she thought she saw a flicker of something outside. She cupped both hands against the windowpane and peered out. She was jumpier than usual tonight, and with each passing moment, her mind ran wild, creating shapes and shadows out of nothing.

You're being paranoid.

Go to bed.

Paranoid or not, she checked the door lock one more time and every latch on every window, confirming everything was secure.

She climbed into bed, staring at the ceiling for a time, thinking.

You're safe. Go to sleep, one part of her mind whispered.

Don't fall asleep. Stay awake. You're in danger, whispered the other.

45

Warm fingers caressed their way down the side of Quinn's cheek, and her eyes flickered open. "Mom, what are you doing here? What time is it?"

"Almost nine o'clock."

She'd slept for several hours, her body succumbing at long last to all the nights she'd spent feeling restless, staring at the ceiling, unable to sleep.

Last night, she'd slept a solid seven hours.

She almost felt normal again.

Her mother pointed to a chair by the window. "Your father's here too."

Quinn looked around. "Where's Jacob? Is he okay?"

"He's in the house with Astrid, having breakfast. It's okay, dear. You've been through a lot. We didn't want to wake you."

Quinn nodded and then shifted her attention to her father. "I'm sorry about your car, Dad."

"Don't worry about the car," he said. "Tell us what happened."

Deciding just how much information to divulge was a slippery slope. Too little and they'd seek additional facts elsewhere.

Too much, and it wouldn't matter how old she was—she'd be lucky if they let her out of their sight until the investigation was over.

Why worry them when the truth was open to interpretation?

Quinn sat up, folding her hands in her lap. "I may have been driving too slow last night. The GPS wasn't working right. There was a truck behind me. The driver seemed impatient and passed me, hitting me in the process."

Simple and to the point, though not well received. Her mother looked at her father. His eyes were damp, his head shaking back and forth like he knew there was more to the story, more she wasn't telling it.

"You should have woken us when you got home," he said.

"I figured it could wait until morning. I'm fine. Just a few bruises to add to the ones that are already there. I tried calling you both last night. When you didn't pick up, I called Astrid. Everything is going to be fine."

"It's not *fine*, Quinn," her father said. "Your sister told me—"

"You know Astrid. She tends to exaggerate. She wasn't there when it happened. There's no telling why I was hit. For all we know, it was an accident."

"Except we don't know it was an accident. We don't know anything." He leaned forward, resting his hands on his knees. "If you're in trouble, you need to tell us. You can only poke a hornet's nest for so long before you get stung."

46

Quinn yanked the shower curtain open in one explosive swoop. Astrid hopped back, her feet sliding across the slickness of the tub as she grappled to regain her balance.

"Why did you talk to Mom and Dad about last night?" Quinn asked. "It wasn't your story to tell."

Astrid dipped her hair under the running water, combing the conditioner out with her fingers. Then she turned the shower off and stepped out, wrapping a towel around her. "I told them because I'm worried about you, okay? You shouldn't be out there trying to solve Evie's murder all by yourself."

"I'm taking precautions. My life is my business."

Astrid went quiet, looking at Quinn, her eyes distant and empty like she was lost.

"We need to make peace with the past," Quinn said.

"Maybe not now, not with all you're going through, but yeah, we should."

"A couple of weeks ago my life was ordinary. The same routine, day in and day out. The highlight of my day was deciding what I was going to prepare for dinner. Can you believe it? I don't even like to cook. I've lived in denial for so long, that all of *this*, everything that's happening right now, is all crashing down on me at the same time—it's overwhelming."

"Turn around."

"What?" Quinn asked.

Astrid placed her hands on Quinn's shoulders and spun her around, so they were both facing the mirror. "Look at our reflection. What do you see?"

"I see the two of us."

"Wanna know what I see in myself? Someone who has the ability to be soft but chooses to be hard instead. Someone who could be kind but knows how much easier it is to close herself off, so she does. Someone who's spent the last several years blaming everything on everyone else, so I don't have to take accountability for what I've done."

"Astrid, you don't need to put down on yourself this—"

"No, Quinn. Let's be honest for once. It's your turn. What do you see in yourself?"

"I see ... I don't ... I don't even know myself anymore."

"Mind if I weigh in? The last time I saw you, your face was gray and ashy, like all the life spark you once had was no longer there. Look at it now. Even though you're in pain over Evie's death, your complexion is rosy and full of life. It's like someone dumped water into your flowerpot, giving you a second chance to bloom. It's okay to let Isaiah go now, to give yourself another chance to live a happy life."

Quinn braced her hands against the sides of the counter, fighting back the emotions. "I just miss him every day. It still hurts so much, you know?"

"I know, and it's all my fault for not fixing things and being there for you. It's the reason why I stayed away. I, ahh ... I've never told you this before, but I sent flowers to Isaiah's grave every month."

"That was you? No matter what our differences, it would have meant a lot to me if I'd known."

"Is there any way you'd let me explain why I made the choices I did?"

If there was ever a time to hear it, a moment when the two of them were getting along, this was it.

"I'll try," Quinn said.

Astrid stood still a moment, thinking.

"When I was in the ninth grade, the basketball coach assigned some of the older high school boys to practice with a few of us," Astrid said. "He thought it would up our game, help us play more aggressive as a team. Bo was assigned to work with me."

"Yeah, I remember."

"He was so kind and playful and fun. He treated me different than the other guys did. I didn't feel like some dumb kid when I was with him. I felt like a woman. Most of the time, after practice, Dad came to the gym to pick me up—except once. He got tied up at work, and he sent you."

"I remember."

"When you got there, we were still finishing up, so you came inside, and you and Bo started talking. I saw the spark between you from the start, and it crushed me."

"Crushed you—*why?*"

"I loved Bo. At least, I loved him as much as a fourteen-year-old freshman could love a guy at age fourteen. I convinced myself he felt the same about me—until he saw you, and then he didn't see me anymore. He only saw *you*, only talked about *you*."

"And you became jealous."

Astrid nodded. "I'm sorry. I hated you for it. You could have dated any guy you wanted, and it felt like you stole him away from me."

"How could I have? I never knew you had those feelings for him. You never told me."

"It wouldn't have made a difference. It wasn't long before the two of you fell for each other, and I was brushed to the side, heartbroken."

Though it didn't excuse her behavior, it all made sense in hindsight.

"You toyed with our lives without giving a second thought to the consequences," Quinn said. "You tried to make me think Bo had been inappropriate with you when he hadn't. What you did, Astrid ... it was cruel."

Astrid pressed a hand to her hip. "*Cruel?* If it had been the first time you'd dated a guy I was interested in, maybe. It wasn't. It was the second, and it stung a lot more the second time than the first."

"The *second?* Who was the other guy?"

"Trevor Flanders. I told you how much I liked him, and you ... you dated him anyway."

"I didn't think you were serious. He was three years older than you. I wasn't trying to hurt you, I swear."

"I believe it now, but back then, I convinced myself you knew what you were doing, that you kept going after the same guys I liked for a reason."

"We're sisters. I wouldn't have done that to you."

"Again, I know that now." Astrid opened the bathroom door, stepped into the hall, and turned back. "If I could take it all back, I would. I hope you can forgive me one day, but even if you don't, I hope even more that you and Bo give each other another chance."

47

Quinn sat on her parents' front porch, watching Jacob play with a set of cars she'd bought him. As the cars rolled along the wood-plank floor, Bo pulled to a stop in front of the house, and her heart skipped a beat.

Quinn's emotions were all over the place today. Bo had never gotten back to her the night before. She assumed it was because he was with Simone. And though she didn't deserve to feel hurt that he'd chosen Simone over her, she was hurt—more than she thought possible.

Bo stepped onto the porch and bent down, playing with Jacob for a few minutes. He glanced her way, and the silence felt heavy. Then he looked up and said, "You up for a walk?"

Quinn glanced skyward, her eyes focused on the dense, gray clouds that were forming. "A walk sounds nice, but it looks like it's going to rain."

"I suppose you're right. I like the rain, the way it smells when a storm is coming. Don't you?"

She did, but she didn't like the idea of getting soaking wet.

"How about we take a walk through the park?" Bo asked. "It's not far. If it starts raining, we'll head back."

Live a little, Quinn. It's just water.

"Okay, sure," she said.

Bo looked at Jacob. "What do you say, bud? You want to come for a walk with us?"

Jacob shook his head and gathered up his cars, heading back inside the house.

"Give me a minute," Quinn said. "Okay?"

Bo nodded, and she followed Jacob inside. She found her mother in the kitchen, whistling as she tidied up.

"Bo's here," Quinn said. "He asked Jacob and I to go for a walk, but the little guy here doesn't want to go."

"I have no plans today. Run along. I'll look after him."

"Thanks, Mom."

Quinn grabbing a jacket from the closet in the casita, and they walked to the park—

the same park where she'd first met Evie. Bo's demeanor was different today. He was a lot quieter, and he looked worried.

"I'm sorry I wasn't around for you last night," he said. "I busted my phone, and I couldn't get it replaced until this morning."

"It's all right. *I'm* all right."

"It's not all right. I should have been there for you, and I wasn't."

"I sent you a text message, but I knew you were busy. I didn't expect to hear back."

"I want you to know I wasn't avoiding you. I wouldn't do that."

"It's fine, Bo. As soon as I sent the message, I felt guilty for doing it. I knew you were with Simone, and by texting you, I wasn't being fair to her, or to you."

"You don't need to concern yourself over her."

"Why not?"

"It's over between us."

A drop of water fell from the sky, splashing onto Quinn's cheek.

She flicked it away.

"Can I ask what happened between the two of you?" Quinn asked.

"I don't feel much like talking about it, if you don't mind. I came to talk to you about your night."

"I'm guessing you talked to Kyle."

Bo nodded. "He said someone ran into you, and he thinks it was intentional."

"It might be. I want to believe it wasn't, but gossip has a way of getting around in this town. Maybe someone was trying to send me a warning."

"What happened last night? Where did you go? Who did you see?"

Quinn turned toward him, going over the previous day's events. She told him about the office meeting and about Marissa being a no-show. Then she mentioned the visit she'd had with Janae, stopping at Marissa's parents' house, and then Rowdy's.

When she finished, he said, "I checked with Marissa's parents this morning. She still hasn't come home."

"Oh, no. Something's wrong, Bo."

"I know. I've got a couple of officers out looking for her."

"Do you think ... I mean, what are the odds she's been taken by the same person who killed Evie?"

"It depends on whether there's a connection between the two, a connection other than their working relationship."

"I want to admit something to you," Quinn said. "Right before I went to bed last night, I could have sworn someone was outside, staring at me through the window. I don't know. Maybe I'm going crazy, and I'm seeing things that aren't there."

He ran a hand along his chin, his expression worried.

"I should have checked in with you," he said. "Now, I wish I had."

"It's all right. Hey, have you figured out who slashed Ray's tires?"

Given she suspected Ruby had been involved, she was hoping he'd say no.

"Yeah," he said. "It was Ruby."

"I assumed as much, even though I don't understand when she would have done it. She was with Jacob most of the day, and even though she's known for her crazy antics, I don't see her doing something like that in his presence."

"I should clarify, I don't think Ruby did it herself. I think she talked someone into doing it for her."

"Did she say as much?"

"The devilish grin on her face when she was questioned this morning was confession enough. If she had help, she won't admit to it."

Thunder growled overhead, followed by sheets of rain. As Quinn's clothes became soaked, she struggled to open the umbrella, and then she realized why—it was broken. Bo removed his jacket, holding it over Quinn's head as they turned, sprinting out of the park toward home.

Voice raised, Bo said, "I don't like what happened last night. I don't want anything to happen to you."

"I don't want anything to happen to me, either."

"No, you don't understand. It's more than that. I ... I ..."

She looked up at him. "You what?"

"I love you, Quinn. I always have."

His words hit her like a slap to the face, her body feeling limp as she scrambled to process her feelings in this moment.

Overwhelmed with emotions, she did the first thing that came to mind.

She turned, and she ran.

Bo charged after her, clutching her arm.

As she spun around, she said, "I'm not the same person I was before. So much has changed since we were together. So much we haven't talked about."

Bo reached out, taking her in his arms as he pulled her toward him. His lips pressed against hers, lingering there for a moment in a passionate embrace. Marcus had kissed her many times over the years, but not once had she felt the same tenderness Bo's single kiss delivered.

He cupped her chin in his hand, tilting it toward him as the rain spilled down around them. "I know you, Quinn. The real you. Yesterday, today, tomorrow—you've always been the same to me."

She could have stood there with him forever, her hair soggy, clothes dripping wet, and it wouldn't have mattered, except for one thing—the unwelcome visitor standing in front of her.

48

"This is why you left me," Marcus said. "For *him?*"

He was parked behind Bo's truck, leaning against his car.

"Marcus, it's not what you think," Quinn said.

"Isn't it? How long have the two of you been seeing each other behind my back? How long, Quinn?"

"You've got it all wrong. Let me explain." As the rain came sputtered to an abrupt stop, she said, "I ... we ..."

"*I ... we ...* what," Marcus pressed.

Bo held up his hands. "Hey, take it easy."

Marcus jolted forward, stabbing a finger to Bo's chest.

"Don't flipping tell me to take it easy, man. You have no business putting your lips on *my* wife." He turned, shifting his attention on Quinn. "And *you.* I never would have married you if I knew you were a cheating little harlot. How long has this been going on? Weeks? Months? Years?"

"I won't allow you to speak to her like that," Bo said.

"She's *my* wife. I'll speak to her in whatever way I please. I suggest you stay out of it."

Bo stepped in front of Quinn, creating a barrier between her and Marcus.

"She left you," Bo said. "It's over."

"You want her? Fine. Take her. But first, how about I fill you in on what you're getting yourself into. She was perfect, at first—the perfect woman, the perfect wife. She's good at getting you to fall in love with her. But once she's succeeded, once you're married, it's *game over* when it comes to sex. But *I* took the high road. *I* stayed with her. *I* remained faithful, which now I see was an obvious mistake on my part."

Marcus was right.

It was *game over*.

But not for the reasons he thought.

As soon as they married, the intimacy stopped. Sex became all about the act itself. There was no bonding, no passion, no care. Marcus got what he needed, and he was done with her. She felt small, unseen, and unloved.

"Did you ever consider the fact Quinn wasn't interested because you're not a real man?" Bo asked. "Why would she be interested in sex with a guy who has no clue how to treat a woman?"

Marcus lunged at Bo, his half-hearted attempt to strike Bo with his fist missing by a few inches. Bo seized Marcus' hands, wrenching them behind his back as he shoved him against the car.

"You get one chance to leave," Bo said. "*One.* If I see you anywhere near Quinn again, I won't be just some guy you saw kissing your soon-to-be ex-wife, I'll be Detective McCallister, and I'll arrest you for assault."

Marcus jerked back, ripping the car door open, spewing one last threat Quinn's way. "I'll see to it you get nothing in the divorce. Not one single thing."

"You don't get it, Marcus," Quinn replied. "I don't want anything from you. I never did."

49

Quinn changed clothes and towel-dried her hair, tossing it back into a loose bun. She found Bo in the living room, sitting in front of the electric fireplace.

"Your shirt is soaked," she said. "I'm sure my dad would let you borrow one of his."

"It's nothing the warmth of this fire won't fix. Unless ... you'd like me to go."

Quinn sat beside him. "I like you just where you are."

"Good. Me too."

"Astrid and I had a chat this morning. I wouldn't say things are good between us, but I know why she sabotaged our relationship now. She was in love with you."

Bo ran a hand along his jaw. "I assumed as much. Couldn't think of any other reason she'd do something like that."

"I had no idea she had a crush on you."

"Yeah, well, If she would have been honest with us, all of this could have been avoided."

"Speaking of honesty, Astrid brought up a good point."

"Yeah," he said. "What's that?"

Nervous, Quinn took a deep breath in.

She wanted to speak her truth.

She just wasn't sure she was brave enough to do it.

"There's something I need to tell you," she said, her voice low.

"What is it?"

"Evie and I went to California for spring break right after you and I broke up. I had no expectations about the trip. I just wanted to get my mind off ... well, *you*."

"I'm so sorry about how it all went down back then. If I had to do it all over again, I wouldn't have let you shut me out. I would have stayed, talked to you until we got to the truth."

"You tried talking to me. I wouldn't listen. Anyway, about what I was saying before ... one night during spring break there was a bonfire on the beach. I had way too much to drink. I met Marcus, and to be honest, I don't remember much at all about that night ... like, what happened."

"What do you mean?"

"The next morning, I asked Evie what she remembered, and she said Marcus and I went for a walk on the beach. When she thought I'd been gone for too long, she went looking for me. She found me throwing up in the girls' bathroom. As soon as I saw her, I burst into tears."

"Why? What happened?"

"I told her I'd done something I shouldn't have. A few days later when we returned to Cody, Marcus started calling me. I ignored his calls, at first. I wanted to forget all about spring break, and just ... all of it. But then I ... I ..."

Quinn went quiet, glancing down at her trembling hands.

Bo placed his hand over hers. "Whatever it is, you can tell me."

Another deep breath in and then, "A few weeks after I got home, I found out I was pregnant. I didn't tell Marcus at first. I was embarrassed. All I could think about was how much shame I'd bring to my family when they found out."

"Guessing you told Marcus at some point."

Quinn nodded. "After my initial shock, I called him. Unlike me, he was thrilled with the news, and he suggested we get married. I wanted to wait. We didn't even know each other. But Marcus has never met a challenge he didn't like. When he sees what he wants, he goes after it. He swooped in and proposed. I knew I shouldn't marry him, but part of me felt like I deserved what was happening, like marrying him was penance for my recklessness, I guess."

"I'm sorry."

"No, *I'm* sorry. I think about the woman I was back then—so timid, lost, and confused. If I could go back and tell that girl to grow a backbone and stand up for herself, I would."

"You did, even if it took a little longer than expected. I'm proud of you, Quinn."

He was proud of her.

Maybe it was time for her to be proud of herself.

"What Marcus said earlier when he saw us together, about our sex life ..."

"Look, you don't owe me an explanation."

"I know, but I'm going to give you one anyway. Sex with Marcus was, in a word, transactional. There was no intimacy in it. He wouldn't even kiss me. He just did what he needed to do, and that was it. After a while, I started finding any excuse to avoid sex with him, but sometimes he'd get aggressive, hounding me until I relented."

"I can't imagine how awful it must have been for you."

"I stayed in the marriage for our son. Marcus knew I was unhappy. He said if I ever left him, he'd fight me in court for full custody. He's a powerful man, and I believed him. When Isaiah died, I wanted to leave. I even planned my exit. I just wasn't strong enough to do it, not until now."

"Having a friend like Evie, and your parents ... I can't believe no one intervened."

Quinn crossed one leg over the other. "Oh, they would have. Given we lived in a different state while we were married, it made it easier for me to hide my true feelings. I lied, to myself and everyone else. Evie had her suspicions. She was always trying to get me to open up. My mother did too. I think they weren't sure if my unhappiness was over the loss of my son, or the trouble in my marriage, or both."

"I wanted to reach out to you as soon as I heard about Isaiah, but I didn't know if you'd want to talk to me, and I didn't want to cause you any more pain."

Quinn glanced at wrist, at the tattooed initials inscribed—a cursive I and M with a heart in the middle.

"Do you know what happened?" she asked.

"I heard bits and pieces, but I don't have all the details."

"It was an accident. An unexpected, awful accident. Isaiah was skipping in the backyard. He tripped and fell, hitting his head on the concrete. 9-1-1 was called right away, but it didn't matter. There was nothing they could do. First my son is taken from me, and now Evie. I'm not sure how much more death I can take."

Bo draped an arm around Quinn, pulling her close. "I'm here for you, for whatever you need. Now and always, for as long as you want me."

50

Marissa wrestled against her restraints, seesawing her wrists back and forth along the coarse wood grain of the chair. She'd been at it for hours now, to no avail. The rope wouldn't loosen. It was tied too tight, and even if it hadn't been, even if she'd managed to free even one of her hands, it was too late.

Her captor had just returned.

She'd heard his car humming in the driveway. It ran for several minutes before the engine chugged, and all went quiet. A door opened and closed, sending a wave of anxiety rushing through her.

The house he'd brought her to was unusual, an abandoned, two-story farmhouse, several miles out of town. He'd never taken her there before. Before today, she never knew it existed.

Sitting in the dark, lamenting the predicament she was in, she'd lost track of time. She didn't even know if it was still the same day or not. Her stomach growled, desperate for even the tiniest morsel, and her mouth was parched, bone-dry.

Every sound and every creak fed into her paranoia.

As she tried to make sense of it all, tears gushed down her cheeks. He had always been so kind. So caring. What changed?

The basement door cracked open, and her stomach lurched.

He was coming.

A long, overhead fluorescent light flickered on and off before it lit up the room. She closed her eyes, the blast of white blinding after so many hours in the dark.

Footsteps shuffled down the stairs, stopping three quarters of the way down.

He sat on the edge of an unfinished-wood stair, glancing down at her.

His eyes looked different today, screwy and unusual, and something else—nervous.

She sat straight up, her eyes coming to rest on the Smith & Wesson lying sideways across his lap. He tapped the top of it with a finger, almost like he wanted to draw her attention to it.

But why?

Was this some kind of game?

If it was a game, she sure was tired of playing.

"Why am I here?" she asked. "Why am I tied up? You haven't said a word to me since you left me in this hellhole."

He blinked at her but said nothing.

"How long are you going to keep me here?" she continued. "Answer me!"

"It all depends on you, Marissa."

"I don't understand."

He cocked his head to the side. "Don't you?"

"Why are you doing this to me? This isn't funny!"

"You think I find any part of the predicament you've put me in funny? I don't."

"I haven't *done* anything. And hey, if you think no one's gonna come looking for me, you're wrong. When they check my phone records, they'll see your number."

He dug into his pocket, pulled out a cell phone, and waved it into the air. "You mean *this* phone? This *burner* phone?"

"Let me go. I want to go home."

He wagged a finger. "Utt, utt, uhh. I talk now. You listen. I've been following you. I saw you with Quinn at the cemetery. What did the two of you talk about?"

"Nothing. Work stuff. She's taking over Evie's business, which means we'll be working together."

"Yeah, see ... that's a problem."

"Why?"

"You *know* why. This, what we've been doing, was not supposed to talked about with anyone."

"I didn't."

"Earlier, you said you and Quinn had girl talk, and darlin', girl talk isn't the same thing as work talk, now is it? You're a tease, and I've come to realize I can't trust you. Besides, I'm getting awful tired of cleaning up your messes."

"What messes?"

"How much does Quinn know about us? What have you told her? The truth, Marissa. No lies."

"No one knows a thing, I swear."

"You expect me to believe you didn't say anything about me after the wisecrack you made?"

"It was a joke."

He shook his head. "Naw, I don't believe you."

"I talked to Quinn about Evie's business. That's all, I swear."

"*Don't* play games with me, Marissa."

"You're scaring me. I haven't told anyone about us, just like we agreed. Whatever you think you saw or heard, you're mistaken. Please. I wouldn't lie to you. And listen, I understand why you wanted to keep our relationship quiet at first. But why does it matter now? I'm of legal age of consent. Who cares about our age difference? I love you, and I want to be with you."

He raised a brow, the look on his face one of shock. "You were nothing but an insignificant, temporary plaything. Someone to pass the time."

As the tears rolled down her face, she said, "How could you say a thing like that after what we've shared together?"

He walked over, squatting in front of her. "Maybe you're right, Marissa. Maybe Quinn doesn't know anything. Still, I need to be certain, and right now, I'm not."

He reached out, stroking the side of her face with his hand. The thought of him touching her was something she'd always looked forward to before. Now, he was different, harsh and detached.

"I'd never lie to you," she said. "The time we've spent together has meant everything to me. I just thought … I mean … I was hoping you'd be open to talking about our future together."

"*Our* future?"

"Yeah, why can't we?"

"I warned you about this when we first got together. It was casual, nothing more."

"If you're trying to say I'm the only one who developed feelings, I don't believe you."

He stared at her, saying nothing.

Marissa tried to keep her wits about her, tried to remain calm, even though she couldn't stop shaking.

"I need to tell you something," she said.

"Yeah? What is it?"

"I'm pregnant."

"What? Impossible, you can't be."

"I am."

He jumped up, pacing in front of her. "It's not mine. It can't be. I thought you said you were on the pill."

"I ... uhh ... stopped taking the pill two months ago. I know, I know. I should have told you."

"What have you done? This is bad. This is so, so bad. How could you do this to me?"

"I'm sorry. I didn't want to go to college. I wanted to stay here and be with you. I thought if I got pregnant, we could get married and—"

He held out a hand. "Stop. How do you know you're pregnant?"

She tipped her head toward her purse, the one he'd tossed onto the dirty floor earlier. "The tests are in there. I took three of them just to be sure."

He snatched her purse, digging inside it.

One by one he pulled out the tests, his eyes wide. The expression on his face wasn't what she'd expected. There was no joy, no happiness. There was only disgust, as if he was sickened by it all.

"How far along are you?" he asked.

"I took the tests this week. I can't be more than five or six weeks, I'd guess."

"Good, then there's still time for you to get rid of it."

"I would never abort our baby."

He shook his head. "You don't get it, everything I've done to protect what we have, to protect our secret. *I* killed Evie Richelle."

No.

It wasn't true.

He was lying.

He had to be.

"I ... I ... don't understand," she said. "Why would you?"

"She saw us together."

"What? Where?"

"The night I dropped you off at your car at our meeting place."

"It's not possible. Where we meet, is way out of town."

"Yeah, well, she drove by one night."

"How can you be so sure it was her?" she asked.

"I'd recognize her motorcycle anywhere, and she looked right at me. Next day, she confronted me about it. You may be of age, but you're still in high school. It's a problem."

"So Evie talked to you about us and you—"

"Did what needed to be done before she made a mess of things."

He raised the pistol to the center of Marissa's forehead and pulled back on the hammer. "You understand I have no choice, right? It was never supposed to come to this, Marissa. But now that it has, I can't have any loose ends, even if it means doing something I wish I didn't have to do."

He'd confessed for a reason.

This was the end—*her* end.

There would be no arguing with her parents about college.

No future life for her in Cody.

Not a single moment of joy knowing what it was like to become a mother.

She'd never see her baby.

"Please, I'll do anything you want," she said. "I'll make something up, tell my parents I got pregnant from a one-night stand with a boy I didn't know. I'll fix it. You'll see."

Shaking his head, he said, "You girls. You're all the same. Think you can bat an eyelash, say the right words, twist your lips into a perfect smile, and you'll have us begging at your feet. It isn't gonna happen today, I'm afraid. Not for you."

51

At half past four in the afternoon, Marissa was still missing. And unlike the previous evening, where excuses were made and reality had yet to set in, the panic surrounding her disappearance spread like wildfire.

Quinn was sitting at Marissa's desk at work. The store was closed for the day, as were most stores around on a Sunday, and she'd locked the front doors, as Bo had requested. He also called or sent her a text every hour on the hour, which Quinn thought was a bit much, even though his little check-ins eased her mind, making her feel safe.

Thoughts swirled inside her head.

Was the killer someone she'd suspected, or someone she'd never even considered yet?

Janae was Ray's alibi, but was she telling the truth?

People did stupid things for love.

What if their affair had been going on a lot longer than she'd claimed?

What if Janae was jealous of Ray's relationship with Evie?

Then there was Rowdy.

Why had he acted so strange when she mentioned Marissa hadn't come to the meeting?

And last, but not least ... Marcus.

For him to show up out of the blue the way he had was unusual. He had far too much pride to do a thing like that, so why did he?

Quinn pushed her thoughts to the side as she shifted her focus to Marissa's desk. The desk was, in a word, disheveled—the drawers cluttered with candy wrappers, various containers of eye shadow, and a stack of notebooks. She'd just turned the first page in the second notebook when she discovered a series of doodles penned in ink. The drawings were a series of men's heads. She flipped to the next page, and the doodles changed. This time, they were babies.

The front door rattled, and Quinn looked up, noting the sun had set. It was dusk, and Bo still hadn't returned to retrieve her. She worried about what that meant, or if they had any leads. Had they found Marissa? And if they had, was she alive?

Quinn walked to the door, relieved when she saw Felicity at the door, a drink in each hand.

"What are you doing here?" Quinn asked.

She held two cups into the air. "I have coffee."

"I see."

"I was driving by, and I saw that you were here. Do you need any help?"

"With what?"

"I know you have a lot to learn, and I wanted to offer my support."

At least she was motivated.

Or was she?

Felicity was an odd bird, to say the least, starting with the multitude of colored highlights in her shoulder-length hair. Her current attire consisted of a pair of multicolored Aztec-patterned leggings, a long, bright green button-up shirt, and a pointy pair of metallic flats.

Odd as she was, her eyes were kind, and she struck Quinn as a person she could trust.

"If you're wondering whether I've heard any news about Marissa, I haven't," Quinn said.

Felicity's shoulders sagged. "Shoot. Hey … ahh, I live alone. It was hard enough to be home alone every night since Evie died. Now, with Marissa missing, I'm a little on edge. And I … I don't want to be alone right now. I know we don't know each other yet, but when I saw you here, I guess I hoped you wouldn't mind a little company."

Quinn nodded and let Felicity in, locking the door behind her.

"You're not the only one who's worried," Quinn said.

Felicity handed her a cup of coffee. "What are you doing here if you don't mind me asking?"

"I've been going through Marissa's desk. Bo said something about looking through it when he comes to pick me up, which will be soon. I thought I'd get a head start, see if she left any clues as to her disappearance."

Felicity scanned the desk, her eyes coming to rest on the notebook. "What are these?"

"Drawings, I guess."

She pointed to one of the male heads. "This guy looks a lot like Rowdy."

Felicity was right.

The face shape was the same. So were the eyes and hair.

"Why would she be sketching pictures of Rowdy?" Quinn asked.

Felicity bit down on her lip.

"Felicity," Quinn said, "if there's something you know, now's the time to tell me."

"It's not that I don't want to tell you what I know. It's just ... Marissa asked me to keep it a secret, and I said I would."

"She's missing. Whatever it is, maybe it shouldn't be a secret anymore."

"Well, I think Rowdy and Marissa are together—in a relationship. A *clandestine* relationship."

"What do you mean, you *think*?"

"I've seen her flirt with him before, and once she told me she was involved in a secret relationship with someone, but refused to reveal with whom."

"She didn't mention Rowdy, then?" Quinn asked.

"Well, no. Not in so many words."

"Then why do you assume it's him?"

"He's sweet on her. I figured it had to be him. The thing is, he's older, and I doubt her parents would approve."

Quinn flipped the notebook page. "Any idea why she'd be drawing babies?"

Another pause, and then Felicity leaned in, whispering even though they were alone. "A few days ago, she threw up at work, and then she kept throwing up the rest of the day. I told her if she was sick, she should go home, but she didn't."

"Are you thinking she's pregnant?" Quinn asked.

"Makes sense, doesn't it?"

"If she was involved in a secret relationship with someone, you should have told the police by now," Quinn said. "Why haven't you?"

"I'm worried they'll think Rowdy had something to do with her disappearance, and I know him. He didn't."

"Listen to me. If Rowdy's innocent, he has no reason to be worried."

Quinn reached for her cell phone, stopping when she heard a tapping sound on the office door. Thinking it was Bo, she smiled as she headed over to the door, stopping when she realized it wasn't him.

It was someone else—someone unexpected.

52

Today, Kyle wasn't dressed in his usual work attire. He wore black track pants and a hoodie, which was pulled over his head. He leaned against the opposite side of the glass office door and said, "Hey, Quinn."

"Hey, Kyle. What are you doing here?"

He smiled. "Just got off the phone with one of my fellow officers. They're at Marissa's parents' house."

"Any word?"

"Not yet. It's a shame. They're searching her room for clues, but so far, they haven't found anything. I was driving by, and I saw you were still here. After what happened last night, I expect you're shaken up. I thought I'd check in. You all right?"

"I'm fine. Bo will be here to get me anytime now."

"Might be a little longer than you expected. He's at Marissa's house, trying to calm her mother down, last I heard. Mind if I come in until he gets here, keep you company?"

Kyle tipped his head back and sneezed. A round pendant dangling from a chain around his neck popped out over his shirt. Quinn's eyes narrowed as she took a closer look, and time slowed to a screeching stop.

In the center of the pendant was a lion, paws up.

On the lion's head was a crown, just like the picture Jacob had drawn.

From behind, Felicity said, "Pssst."

Quinn turned.

Ducking behind a tall plant like she was trying to stay out of Kyle's eyeline, Felicity tilted one of Marissa's notebooks just enough for Quinn to notice Felicity's finger pressed onto a sketch of a man Marissa had drawn, a man who now looked a lot more like Kyle than Rowdy.

Quinn glanced outside, assessing her surroundings. The street outside the office was quiet and deserted, the café across the street—closed.

Forcing a smile, Quinn said, "Let me grab the office key, and I'll let you in."

He nodded, and she excused herself, trying not to walk too fast as she made her way toward Felicity.

"Take my cell phone, go into the next room, lock yourself inside, and send Bo a text message," Quinn said. "He's in my contacts. Do not dial 9-1-1 or the police. And no matter what happens, keep quiet until I come back for you, okay?"

Felicity nodded.

Heart racing, Quinn slid Evie's gun into her pocket and returned to the office door. "I could have sworn the keys were in my purse, but they're not there. If you could give me a few minutes, I'm sure I can find them."

"Are you all alone here tonight?" he asked.

"Yep, it's just me."

"I could have sworn I just heard you talking to someone."

Quinn steadied her breath, trying to compose herself. "I was talking to myself, frustrated because ... I, you know, don't know what I did with the key."

She thought she'd been convincing, quick on her feet with her response.

But one look at Kyle's face, and it was clear—he didn't believe her.

53

Kyle tapped the tips of his fingers against the glass. "Go get the key, Quinn, and then let me in. We need to talk."

"It's been a long day, Kyle. Let's talk later, okay?"

"I'd rather talk now. Is something wrong?"

"No, why would it be?"

"The way you're looking at me ... it's different."

"I don't know what you're talking about," Quinn said.

"You're scared. Why? What's changed?"

Unsure what to say, she paused and folded her arms. "It's not you. This whole thing with Evie's murder, and now Marissa's missing ... I've been anxious and apprehensive for days."

"That's why you should let me in. Go on, go get the key."

She took one step, then another, backing away from the door. "It's like I said before, it's been a long day, and I'm tired. I'll catch up with you in the morning."

He narrowed his eyes, gritting his teeth. "All right, Quinn. You've made your decision. Now I'll make mine."

Kyle leaned back and reached for the gun in his holster, a

gun equipped with a silencer. He aimed it at the door and fired, peppering the room with shattered glass.

Quinn turned, sprinting in the other direction.

Unsure of where to go, she ducked into a hallway and pulled the gun from her pocket, trying her best to steady it in her clammy hands.

Kyle stepped inside the office, the heels of his shoes crunching against the shattered glass as he came toward her.

"You're not the only one who's armed, Kyle," Quinn warned.

"Are you saying you'd fire at me? Now, that's funny. You've always been a softie. You won't shoot me. Hell, I doubt you even know how to use the dang thing."

If he thought she wouldn't shoot to kill, he was wrong.

Without thinking it through, she fired a warning shot, regretting the decision as soon as the gun went off.

"Well, well, guess we're about to have ourselves a good, old-fashioned shootout," he said.

"Where's Marissa? What have you done with her?"

"What makes you think I had anything to do with her disappearance?"

"It's been you all along," Quinn said. "You wouldn't have shot your way in here if it wasn't."

"What I want to know is, when did you figure out I was the one who killed Evie?"

The office lights switched off, the only illumination filtering into the room coming from a lamppost outside. Quinn remained still, listening, trying to place him.

Kyle's breath was thick and heavy. He was close by, several feet away, Quinn guessed, and closing in. He'd round the corner anytime now and take a shot. If she was going to make a move, she needed to do it.

Closer still he came, and the floor creaked, giving away his precise location.

Quinn leapt forward.

Rounding the corner, she fired.

Kyle bellowed in pain, and she heard what sounded like someone dropping to the ground.

Had she wounded him?

Was he dead?

Was he bluffing?

She'd taken a single shot in the dark.

She'd be a fool to assume she'd killed him on her first try.

Seconds passed, seconds that felt like hours, Quinn doing her best to keep quiet as she backed into the hallway, inching her way little by little until she reached the end.

There was nowhere else to go, and no way out.

Seconds later, she heard movement.

Kyle was alive, the sounds she heard indicating he was crawling toward her. A gunshot rang out, the bullet narrowly missing her face. And then another. This time the bullet connected, clipping her arm. She smacked a hand against her mouth, trying her best not to scream, but the pain was too excruciating.

"Come on now, Quinn," he said. "I have you cornered. Talk to me. Tell me what you know. Aren't you curious about why Evie had to die? Or have you figured that out too?"

Stay where you are.

Make no moves.

Say nothing.

Quinn smoothed her fingers over her neck until she felt the metal from Evie's necklace in her hands. It made her feel stronger somehow, like she wasn't fighting him alone.

"Guess you could call Evie 'the woman who knew too much,'" he joked. "Wrong place, wrong time. Didn't want to do it. Honest. I had no choice. Then again, she was always nosey, like a curious cat, and sometimes cats need to be put down for their own good."

He entered the hallway, his face coming into view for a split second, but a second was all she needed. She jerked her foot back, slamming the heel of her boot into his groin. The gun slipped from his hands. He reached for it, and as he wrapped it around his fingers and aimed at her head, she smiled, and then she took her revenge.

54

A drone of sirens vibrated through the town's sleepy streets. Quinn remained still, in the same spot where she'd collapsed minutes before, trying to hold back the tears as the reality of the night's events came crashing down around her.

Felicity was by her side now, wrapping Quinn's arm with gauze she'd found in a first aid kit in the bathroom.

Vehicles screeched to a stop outside, doors opening and closing. Then she heard Bo's booming voice, calling out to her as people filed into the room.

"Quinn," Bo yelled. "Where are you?"

Felicity responded for her. "Here! She's here!"

The moment Bo's face came into view, a wave of relief swept over Quinn, and she could contain her tears no longer.

He dropped to his knees, assessing her all over, including the wound she'd sustained.

"I tried to wrap it the best way I could," Felicity said. "But I've never done it before."

"You did great," Bo said. "I'm glad you were here and that the two of you are safe."

"I'm ... I .. I killed him, Bo," Quinn said. "I shot him. I had no choice. He would have killed me if I hadn't. He killed Evie, and I'm afraid he did the same to Marissa."

"It's all right. Right now, we need to get you to the hospital."

Quinn was lifted onto a stretcher, wheeled outside, and guided with care into the ambulance. Bo hopped in the with her, nodding at the EMT in the driver's seat as he said, "We're in. Let's go."

As the ambulance took off, Bo reached out, grabbing Quinn's hand and pressing it to his lips. "I'm here, babe. I'm right here. I got you."

"I need to tell you ... need to tell—"

"What happened back there can wait, all right? Let's focus on you right now."

"No ... I ... need ... to ... tell ... you ...need to tell you ... I love you too, Bo."

55

"I don't think we can take another scare like this, sweetie," Quinn's father said.

Quinn looked up, smiling at her family who'd gathered around her hospital bed. Her father, her mother, her sister. It felt good to have them there.

"Where's Jacob?" Quinn asked. "I don't want him to see me like—"

Quinn's mother reached out, taking her hand. "He's just fine, sweetie. He's with Ruby."

"Oh, good. Where's—"

"Bo?" her father said with a wink. "He'll be right back. The cafeteria didn't have any food he thought you'd like. He left to get you something better."

A young nurse with short, dark, curly hair, wearing Daffy Duck scrubs entered the room. "Hey, how are you feeling, hun?"

Quinn looked at the sling on her arm. "Better now that I'm all patched up. Am I free to go?"

"The doctor will be coming in to talk to you. After that, if he's happy with everything, I'll bring you some paperwork, and you should be on your way. I'll let him know you're awake."

The nurse walked out, and Bo walked in, carrying a bag from Quinn's favorite burger place.

Quinn's father thumbed at the door, looking at her mother and sister as he said, "Let's give these two some alone time, shall we?"

They walked out, and Bo approached the bed, leaning down to kiss Quinn on the forehead.

"Hi," he said.

"Hi."

"You hungry?"

"I'm starving."

He pulled up a chair and reached into the bag, pulling out a burger and fries and setting them on the tray in front of her.

"Have you found Marissa?" Quinn asked.

"Before I say anything, let me look at you—really look at you. I don't think I've allowed myself to do it until now."

"You can look at me for the rest of my life, if you like. But right now, I'm anxious to know if you've found anything out."

"You're a hard woman to say no to, do you know that?"

"I'm aware," she said. "You were saying?"

They both laughed.

"Kyle's grandparents had a farmhouse outside town," he said. "They've both passed away, and it's been sitting there abandoned, for years. Figured it would be the perfect place for him to take Marissa, and I was right."

"Is she ... dead?"

He nodded, and Quinn's heart sank.

"We found her tied to a chair in the basement," he said. "Right before he came to see you last night, he'd stopped by Marissa's parents. I thought nothing of it at the time. He was in Marissa's room for a few minutes with one of the other officers, and I'm guessing he came across a diary Marissa kept. We found it stashed under the spare tire in the back of his car."

Quinn tried sitting up and winced.

"Here, let me help," Bo said.

She nodded, and he wrapped an arm around her, boosting her up.

"What did she write about in the diary?" Quinn asked.

"The diary proves Kyle had been in a sexual relationship with Marissa for several months."

"I found a notebook in her desk at the office with doodles of Kyle and a baby. Felicity told me Marissa had thrown up at work. Was she pregnant?"

Bo hung his head, giving Quinn the answer.

"She thought getting pregnant would keep her parents from sending her to college," he said, "something she also wrote about it in the diary."

"'m surprised he got involved with her in the first place given things have a way of getting out in this town."

Bo was right.

Evie had discovered Kyle's liaison with Marissa, and she was murdered because of it.

"Right before Kyle died, he said Evie was the woman who knew too much," Quinn said. "It hurts knowing she was killed over his stupid affair."

"Guess he thought if he removed the threats, he'd remove the blame. He didn't see you coming, though."

"He remembered me as a sweet pushover. Still, it doesn't explain who ran into me the night I left Rowdy's house."

"At the farmhouse, I found an old pickup covered with a tarp in the garage. It was gray and white, and it had some damage to the door panel on the right side. I'm guessing it'll be a match to the paint embedded on the side of your father's car."

"But Kyle showed up that night, in a different car."

"You know as well as I do that he was born and raised here. He could have easily stashed the truck somewhere no one would see it and then returned for it later. Wouldn't surprise me one bit."

"I can't believe it's over."

"Me either, but I hope it gives you the closure you need to move on."

Moving on ...

"Uhh ... about what I said in the ambulance last night," she said. "You heard me, right?"

Bo took her hand in his, looking her in the eye. "I sure did, and I can promise you one thing, I'll never allow anything to come between us again."

56

Nine Months Later

Quinn folded her hand inside Jacob's, and they strolled along the grassy path.

"Have I ever told you this park was where I met your mother when we were kids?" she asked.

"Yeah," he said, nodding.

Lifting a finger, she pointed. "It was on that swing right over there."

Though the park had been maintained over the years, decades of consistent use had worn down almost all the equipment on the playground. Rusted slides. Eroded flecks of rubber on the swings. To preserve Evie's memory, Quinn had created a fundraiser. The amount raised was substantial, enough to revitalize the park with an array of modernized equipment, benches, and even a lighted gazebo.

Looking at the changes being put into place now, she was

proud of the achievement, proud of the way she'd turned her life around in less than a year's time. Four months earlier, she'd purchased her own place, a two-story Victorian she'd just begun renovating. And thanks to Rowdy, her new business partner, her thumb had become a lot greener.

With each passing day, Jacob seemed more and more like himself.

And then there was Bo. A month before, he'd talked about their future together, a future they'd already started to plan. With her divorce almost final, she looked forward to the day Bo would get down on one knee and they'd begin their amazing life together.

And though Isaiah and Evie were constant on her mind, she also tried focusing on the here and now, on the things she could change. Today the "here and now" meant spending the day with Jacob.

They approached the swings, and she said, "Want me to push you?"

"Okay, not too high, okay?"

Quinn knelt, meeting him at eye level. Wrapping her hands around his waist, she looked him in the eye, reciting a familiar line someone had once said to her. "Don't worry, sweetheart. When you're with me, I won't ever let anything bad happen to you."

EPILOGUE

In the two days Natalie had stayed at the manor, Margaret had only seen her on a couple of occasions. In both instances, Natalie had the book Margaret recommended in hand, which pleased Margaret. She hoped within the book's pages, Natalie's heart would open to the idea of mending her relationship with Bronte.

As Margaret shuffled around the table, setting out the quiche of the day, a few of the manor's guests entered the room. They greeted each other, chitchatting a moment before taking a seat at the table. Margaret had hoped today Natalie would join them, unlike the past two days when she'd chosen to remain in her room.

Returning to the kitchen to fetch a pitcher of orange juice, Margaret was met with a pleasant surprise when she reentered the dining room and saw Natalie sitting among the other guests. The book Margaret had given her to read was resting in her lap.

Natalie looked over at Margaret and smiled, saying, "Good morning."

"Good morning to you," Margaret replied. "Have you enjoyed your stay, dear?"

"I have."

"And the book ... have you read it?"

Natalie grabbed the book and handed it to Margaret. "I finished it last night."

"What do you think of it?"

"I *think* I understand why you gave it to me. It's given me a lot to consider."

"Oh?"

Margaret wanted to press Natalie for more information, but not knowing if Natalie would want to discuss the situation in front of the other guests, she remained quiet. If Natalie wanted to share her circumstances with them, it was her choice to do so.

As if reading her mind, Natalie looked at the other guests and said, "I came here for a couple of days because I've been having a hard time with my college roommate and good friend, Bronte. I was telling Margaret about it when I first arrived, and she recommended a book from her library, *Eye for Revenge*."

She held the book up for everyone to see.

A man sitting across from Natalie said, "May I ask what's it about?"

"Murder, amateur sleuthing, giving love a second chance, and most of all—friendship."

"Ahh, it sounds interesting."

"The book is about a woman who learns her childhood friend has been murdered. She returns to the town she grew up in to seek out the killer, and in doing so, she starts to rebuild her life. It made me think a lot about my behavior over the past few weeks, and how poorly I've handled the situation with Bronte. I thought about how I'd feel if lost her, and ... well, I realized life is too short to argue with a friend who's always been there for me in life."

Pleased, Margaret clapped her hands together, smiling. "I'm glad to hear it."

"And I'm glad I came here. It's just what I needed."

"Have you had the chance to talk to Bronte since you've been here?"

"Not yet. But, speaking of that ..." Natalie stood, grabbing a napkin and a piece of toast off a plate. "If you'll all excuse me, I have an important phone call to make."

THE END

THANK YOU

Thank you for reading Eye for Revenge, book 1 in the Margaret Montague mystery series. I hope you enjoyed getting to know the characters in this story as much as I enjoyed writing them for you.

In THE KILLING HOUR (Margaret Montague, Book 2)

Suburban housewife Juliette Granger has been living a secret life ... a life that's about to turn deadly.

After witnessing a brutal killing, Juliette grabs her three-year-old daughter, Nora, and disappears into the night, determined to vanish to a quiet town under a new name. An hour down the highway, headlights fill her rearview mirror. A masked man pulls alongside, ordering her to stop. When Juliette hits the gas instead, the night explodes into a deadly pursuit that will change the lives of everyone she loves forever.

A USA Today Bestselling Book

Here's a sneak peek of Chapter One ...

...

THE KILLING HOUR

J uliette Granger glanced in the car's rearview mirror once more, a knee-jerk reaction she couldn't stop repeating, even though no matter how many times she looked, there was nothing to indicate she was being followed. She'd been driving the desert stretch between Las Vegas and St. George, Utah, for the last hour, and given it was the middle of the night, fellow motorists were sparse at best. Even so, she felt nauseous and unsettled—unable to shake the feeling that as soon as her husband Seth realized she was gone, he would do everything in his power to find her.

For now, Juliette took comfort in her biggest ally—time. She'd slipped out of the house an hour and a half earlier as soon as Seth began snoring. Taking every precaution not to rouse him, she'd inched her hand beneath the bed, retrieving a bag she'd hidden earlier in the day while he was out running errands. In that moment, she'd glanced over at Seth before sliding out of bed, horrified when she noticed he had rolled over.

And that wasn't all.

One of his eyes had slid open, and he appeared to be looking at her.

She couldn't move, couldn't breathe, transfixed by the steady rhythm of his chest. Then, with a sudden roll, he turned, and the rasp of his snoring filled the room once more.

Juliette had been planning her exit for the past two weeks.

New place.

New people.

Somewhere safe.

Somewhere no one would think to look.

And most of all, somewhere *he* wouldn't find her.

The buzz of her cell phone on the passenger seat jolted Juliette back to the present, a sharp prickle racing across her skin.

What if it's him?

She hesitated and then flipped the phone to see who was calling, exhaling a sigh of relief as she brought the phone to her ear. "Hey, sis."

"Hey, how's it going?"

"Everything's fine so far."

"Did you make it out all right?"

"Yeah."

"Good. Where are you now?"

Juliette glanced up at a billboard advertising a prime-rib special at a nearby casino. "I'm just getting into Mesquite."

"You shouldn't be too much longer then. I'll let you go so you can concentrate on driving."

Juliette gripped the steering wheel, her mind racing. "Wait, are you still there?"

"Yeah, I'm here."

"I'm worried I made the wrong decision."

"I know how hard this was for you, but if you're unhappy, it was the right call."

"It's just ... I'm scared."

"It's normal to feel this way when you're making such a big change. What did Seth say when you talked to him?"

"I ... umm, I didn't talk to him. I tried to at dinner, but I chickened out. Even now, just thinking about it, my stomach is in knots, and I feel like I can't breathe. I thought about pulling into a gas station and grabbing a soda or something fizzy to settle my nerves, but I think I should keep going."

"Making a pit stop wouldn't take long, maybe five minutes. You should do it."

Juliette wanted to, but the idea seemed like too big of a risk.

She had to keep going.

"I'm ... I'll be fine. Once Seth wakes up, once he realizes I'm gone, he'll come looking for me."

"I hate to say this, but he deserves an explanation, Juliette."

"I know. I left a note. It's not how I intended it to go, but it's better than no explanation at all."

"What did the note say?"

"I told him I was sorry for walking out the way I did. I told him I didn't want to be married anymore, and I asked him not to come after me." Juliette exhaled, her voice heavy. "Maybe I shouldn't have dragged you into the situation. My marriage is my burden, not yours."

"It's not *your* problem. It's *our* problem. You're my baby sister. I just wish you would have told me about your marital problems sooner. I knew you were struggling, but I didn't realize how bad things had gotten."

"I wanted to tell you. I thought about it whenever we talked on the phone. I shouldn't have waited so long. I'm sorry."

If she could do it over, she would have told her sister everything from the beginning—everything but the truth about how she'd been living these past four years. But that was out of the question.

Raine had believed Juliette was coming to stay for a while, but she wasn't. She'd come to say goodbye—perhaps for good.

"Don't be sorry," Raine said. "I should be the one apologizing, not you. I've been so caught up in my own life, I haven't been there for you, not in the way I should have. You're a lot stronger than you think. You'll get through this in time. I know you will."

Juliette wasn't so sure.

"I feel like everything's a haze," Juliette said. "My life's a mess. I've made so many mistakes. You have no—"

Idea.

She stopped herself before saying it, knowing the admission might prompt Raine to ask questions she didn't want to answer.

"It's going to be all right," Raine said. "Trust me. How's Nora doing?"

Juliette looked over her shoulder at her three-year-old, snug beneath a blanket in her car seat. "She's asleep. She's got her unicorn, the one you gave her."

"What did you tell her?"

"I said we were going on a trip. She asked where, and I said it was a surprise. She hopped out of bed, grabbed her blanket and her unicorn, and ran to the front door."

"I can't wait to see you both."

"Raine?"

"Yeah?"

"I love you."

"I love you too. See you soon, okay?"

"Yeah, see you soon."

...

Order your copy of The Killing Hour today at CherylBradshawStore.Com (and a big thank you to all those who order direct from the store—it is appreciated). You can also order it at your preferred retailer store.

ENJOY EYE FOR REVENGE?

You can show your appreciation by leaving a review on Amazon, Barnes & Noble, Apple Books, Google Play, Kobo, or Goodreads. If you write a review, please be sure to email Cheryl (cheryl@authorcherylbradshaw(dot)com) so she can express her gratitude. She does her best to reply to as many emails as she can, and she appreciates every piece of mail she receives.

ABOUT CHERYL BRADSHAW

Cheryl Bradshaw is a New York Times and 16-time USA Today bestselling author writing in multiple genres, including mystery, thriller, romantic suspense, supernatural suspense, and poetry. She is a Shamus Award finalist for best private eye novel of the year, an eFestival of Words winner for best thriller, and has published over fifty books since 2011.

When she's not writing, Cheryl loves jet-setting to new countries, playing with her grandkids, high tea, and pursuing a wishful side career as a professional food tester of wine and cheese.

NEVER MISS ONE OF
CHERYL'S BOOK'S AGAIN!

Sign up for Cheryl Bradshaw's "Killer Newsletter" today to be the first to know when a new book is released and to enter to win fun bookish swag. You'll also receive some fantastic book freebies just for joining!

Learn more by visiting CherylBradshawStore.Com and filling out your email address on the SIGN UP AND SAVE form at the bottom of the home page.

BOOKS BY CHERYL BRADSHAW

Sloane Monroe Series

Silent as the Grave (Prequel, Book 0)

When the body of Rebecca Barlow is found floating in the lake, private investigator Sloane Monroe takes on her very first homicide.

Black Diamond Death (Book 1)

Charlotte Halliwell has a secret. But before revealing it to her sister, she's found dead.

Murder in Mind (Book 2)

A woman is found murdered, the serial killer's trademark "S" carved into her wrist.

I Have a Secret (Book 3)

Doug Ward has been running from his past for twenty years. But after his fourth whisky of the night, he doesn't want to keep quiet, not anymore.

Stranger in Town (Book 4)

A frantic mother runs down the aisles, searching for her missing daughter. But little Olivia is already gone.

Bed of Bones (Book 5) (USA Today Bestselling Book)

Sometimes even the deepest, darkest secrets find their way to the surface.

Flirting with Danger (Book 5.5) A Sloane Monroe Short Story

A fancy hotel. A weekend getaway. For Sloane Monroe, rest has finally arrived, until the lights go out, a woman screams, and Sloane's nightmare begins.

Hush Now Baby (Book 6) (USA Today Bestselling Book)

Serena Westwood tiptoes to her baby's crib and looks inside, startled to find her newborn son is gone.

Dead of Night (Book 6.5) A Sloane Monroe Short Story

After her mother-in-law is fatally stabbed, Wren is seen fleeing with the bloody knife. Is Wren the killer, or is a dark, scandalous family secret to blame?

Gone Daddy Gone (Book 7) (USA Today Bestselling Book)

A man lurks behind Shelby in the park. Who is he? And why does he have a gun?

Smoke & Mirrors (Book 8) (USA Today Bestselling Book)

Grace Ashby wakes to the sound of a horrifying scream. She races down the hallway, finding her mother's lifeless body on the floor in a pool of blood. Her mother's boyfriend Hugh is hunched over her, but is Hugh really her mother's killer?

Sloane Monroe Stories: Deadly Sins

Deadly Sins: Sloth (Book 1)

Darryl has been shot, and a mysterious woman is sprawled out on the floor in his hallway. She's dead too. Who is she? And why have they both been murdered?

Deadly Sins: Wrath (Book 2)

Headlights flash through Maddie's car's back windshield, someone following close behind. When her car careens into a nearby tree, the chase comes to an end. But for Maddie, the end is just the beginning.

Deadly Sins: Lust (Book 3)

Marissa Calhoun sits alone on a beach-like swimming hole nestled on Australia's foreshore. Tonight, the lagoon is hers and hers alone. Or is it?

Deadly Sins: Greed (Book 4)

It was just another day for mob boss Giovanni Luciana until he took his car for a drive.

Deadly Sins: Envy (Book 5)

A cryptic message. A missing niece. And only twenty-four hours to pay.

Deadly Sins: Pride (Book 6)

A secret lies within the Kingston mansion's walls, a secret that's about to bring the past into the present.

Deadly Sins: Gluttony (Book 7)

In a town where silence holds its own dark voice, the past has returned, and Gideon Belmont about to learn an unfortunate lesson. Someone has been harboring a grudge, and for Gideon, endings don't come easy in a town that never forgets.

Sloane & Maddie, Peril Awaits (Co-Authored with Janet Fix)

The Silent Boy (Book 1)

In the hallway of a local tavern, six-year-old Louie Alvarez waits for his mother to take him home. A scream rips through the air, followed by the sound of a gun being fired. Louie freezes, then turns, with a single thought on his mind: RUN.

The Shadow Children (Book 2)

Within the tunnels of the historic port city of Savannah, fourteen-year-old Andi Leland has her mind set on freedom—not just for herself but for all the other teens who have come before her.

The Broken Soul (Book 3)

When the party of a lifetime becomes a party to the death, the lines become blurred. Friends become enemies. Drugs become weapons. And that's just the beginning.

The Widow Maker (Book 4)

A friend murdered. A business in trouble. A marriage struggling to survive. And that's just the beginning.

The Familiar Stranger (Book 5)

As semi-retired private detective Sloane Monroe unwinds at a luxurious spa retreat in North Carolina, a jarring phone call shatters her peaceful getaway ...

Georgiana Germaine Series

Little Girl Lost (Book 1)

For the past two years, former detective Georgiana "Gigi" Germaine has been living off the grid, until today, when she hears some disturbing news that shakes her.

Little Lost Secrets (Book 2)

When bones are discovered inside the walls during a home renovation, Georgiana uncovers a secret that's linked to her father's untimely death thirty years earlier.

Little Broken Things (Book 3)

Twenty-year-old Olivia Spencer sits at her desk in her mother's bookshop, dreaming about her upcoming wedding. The store may be closed, but she's not alone, and her dream is about to become her worst nightmare.

Little White Lies (Book 4)

When a serial killer sweeps through the streets of Cambria, California, Georgiana Germaine gets swept up into a tangled web of deception and lies.

Little Tangled Webs (Book 5)

What if you knew the person you loved was murdered, but no one else believed you? Eighteen-year-old Harper Ellis knows she's right, and she's prepared to risk her life to prove it.

Little Shattered Dreams (Book 6)

At fifty-five, Quinn Abernathy has been through her fair share of experiences in life. And tonight, her past is coming back to haunt her.

Little Last Words (Book 7)

After living in a verbally abusive relationship for the past six years, twenty-seven-year-old Penelope Barlow has finally found the courage to leave. But can she escape ... with her life?

Little Buried Secrets (Book 8)

In a split-second, a car collides with Margot, and she finds herself hurdling through the air, her bike going one way as she goes the other. Her mind whirls in this moment, as she thinks about her life and just how much she doesn't want to die.

Little Stolen Memories (Book 9)

In a secluded cabin deep within the woods, an ominous stranger is about to change the lives of six unsuspecting teenagers forever.

Little Empty Promises (Book 10)

As librarian Cordelia Bennett prepares to lock up for the night, a mysterious sound startles her. She turns. The fading light reveals a chilling presence in the shadows, and Cordelia realizes she's not alone.

Little Hidden Fears (Book 11)

Noelle Winters has just thrown the perfect engagement party ... or so she believes. As the evening winds down and the toast is about the commence, the lights go out. And for someone, the night has just turned deadly.

Little Dark Deeds (Book 12)

It's Georgiana Germaine's wedding day. But when one of her closest friends is noticeably absent from the ceremony, Georgiana worries something sinister is to blame.

Little Silent Stranger (Book 13)

A quiet walk through the woods. A secret left unspoken. A murder that tears through a small town and everyone in it.

Margaret Montague Series

Eye for Revenge (Book 1) USA Today Bestselling Book

Quinn Montgomery wakes to find herself in the hospital. Her childhood best friend Evie is dead, and Evie's four-year-old son witnessed it all. Traumatized over what he saw, he hasn't spoken.

The Killing Hour (Book 2) USA Today Bestselling Book

Suburban housewife Juliette Granger has been living a secret life ... a life that's about to turn deadly.

Addison Lockhart Series

Grayson Manor Haunting (Book 1)

When Addison Lockhart inherits Grayson Manor after her mother's untimely death, she unlocks a secret that's been kept hidden for over fifty years.

Rosecliff Manor Haunting (Book 2)

Addison Lockhart jolts awake. The dream had seemed so real. Eleven-year-old twins Vivian and Grace were so full of life, but they couldn't be. They've been dead for over forty years.

Blackthorn Manor Haunting (Book 3)

Addison Lockhart leans over the manor's window, gasping when she feels a hand on her back. She grabs the windowsill to brace herself, but it's too late-- she's already falling.

Belle Manor Haunting (Book 4)

A vehicle barrels through the stop sign, slamming into the car Addison

Lockhart is inside before fleeing the scene. Who is the driver of the other car? And what secrets within the walls of Belle Manor will provide the answer?

Crawley Manor Haunting (Book 5)

Something evil is coming. Something dark. Something seeking to destroy everything and everyone in its path. And Addison Lockhart is the only one who can stop it.

Till Death do us Part Novella Series

Whispers of Murder (Book 1)

It was Isabelle Donnelly's wedding day, a moment in time that should have been the happiest in her life...until it ended in murder.

Echoes of Murder (Book 2)

When two women are found dead at the same wedding, medical examiner Reagan Davenport will stop at nothing to discover the identity of the killer.

Stand-Alone Novels

The Perfect Lie

When true-crime writer Alexandria Weston is found murdered on the last stop of her book tour, fellow writer Joss Jax steps in to investigate.

Hickory Dickory Dead (USA Today Bestselling Book)

Maisie Fezziwig wakes to a harrowing scream outside. Curious, she walks outside to investigate, and Maisie stumbles on a grisly murder that will change her life forever.